Atkinson's Adversary

The Reaper Series

Book Three

John Paul Bernett

JOHN PAUL BERNETT

ISBN: 978-0-9926173-2-5

Acknowledgements

I would like to thank Gavin Johnson & Lee Coates of V-Edition Media for the superb work on the cover design.

Also as ever, many thanks to my wife Beverly Gail Bernett for all her tireless editing.

And thanks to Deborah Priestley Photography for a great author photograph.

JOHN PAUL BERNETT

The Dark Realm

When the soul leaves the body, it begins its journey from the Realm of Death to its next existence. This is the way of most souls that pass through the Realm of the Reaper (the Realm of Death). If, however, you are one of the unfortunate souls who has not lived a good life and has caused damage to another animal or the planet, your soul is stripped of your life force, and your individual journey has come to an end. Your soul is placed in storage for the next dominant species.

Sadly, with the ways that humanity has behaved, there are more and more of these surplus souls, and the realm where they are stored is filling up. Thousands of years' worth of tormented souls, all in one place – and all wanting revenge on the God that put them there.

Abandon hope, all ye who enter the Dark Realm.

JOHN PAUL BERNETT

JOHN PAUL BERNETT

In the darkest of places, the smallest spark of light can offer you the illumination that you need to carry on

Chapter One

As Gavin's Jaguar sports car raced towards the Maternity Ward of the hospital where they both worked, he glanced across at Sarah. She was breathing deeply, and starting to show that she was very distressed.

"I will have you there soon, Sarah," said Gavin.

"No! Stop the car, there's something wrong! Call Tamara!" screamed Sarah.

The XK120 screeched to a halt, leaving smoking tyre trails behind the back wheels. Gavin depressed Tamara's button on his phone. Instantly, they were transported to Listmaker.

"What has happened?" asked Tamara.

"She started breathing heavily and wanting to push, but it's too early!" replied Gavin.

"I was expecting this," said Tamara.

"But she is only seven months..."

"I know, let's have her here with me. Come on little one – we are going to a familiar place," said Tamara as Sarah fell unconscious. "You come too, Gavin, we may need you. She cannot possibly have this baby in human form. It would mean the end of both mother and child."

Tamara picked up her sister with one arm and took hold of Gavin with her other hand. Within seconds, they were in a different realm, and all three were in warrior mode but bereft of weapons. Sarah returned to consciousness. Her pain and distress had left her. She gazed into her sister's eyes and said, "Why are we here, Tamara?"

"Because, little one, you nearly had your baby early, and you were going to deliver him in human form – which would not have been a good idea."

"I didn't realise that," said Sarah.

"Yes sister, to have this baby, you need to be in warrior mode, and there is only one midwife capable of delivering this wonderful creation that you are nurturing," informed Tamara.

All three of them walked down a leafy path with weeping willows creating a parasol against the sunlight. Above them, birds were whistling in the trees, and the sounds of frogs croaked from the stream at their side.

The dappled spots of light danced along the stream that paralleled the path that they walked; the gentle forest sounds were soothing to Sarah's ears. The three Warriors came to a clearing where an old woman stood. Although elderly, she was beautiful; her skin showed no wrinkles, her long white hair parted in the middle and flowed down to and over her shoulders then down her back. Her hair was adorned with all kinds of natural trinkets – such as feathers, pearls and jewels. Her white gown was long and elegant, and shimmered in the dappled light. She wore a headdress, again made from natural things, such as feathers and flowers.

At her feet was an array of small animals, and hummingbirds, dragonflies and butterflies hovered around her head. In her left hand she held a long staff with a crystal at its top and ancient writing along its shaft; she held out her other hand to Sarah. Sarah's face lit up as Tamara knelt down on one knee, and said, "Mother, behold your daughter, with the unborn child."

The woman took hold of Sarah's hands, and the two giants embraced. Sarah immediately felt at ease. Her anguish was gone, and all thoughts of anxiety had left her.

She was, in fact, at one with Mother Nature herself. A feeling of elation filled her entire being; the same feeling transferred to Gavin and Tamara.

After a while, the immense euphoric feeling within that open circle in the middle of the woods, within the Realm of Nature, was replaced by a sense of calm. It was a feeling of safety...of a new beginning, and a bright future. It was as if Nature had provided a saviour. This star-child hybrid of everything good about humanity and the strongest power in the Realm of Nature would become the bringer of joy to the world.

"Would you like to see your baby?" asked the woman.

In a slightly dazed state, Sarah smiled, and nodded her head. Mother Nature also smiled as in the middle of the group a mist appeared. It began to swirl and then cleared. In its stead was a baby, turning slightly in a circular motion in front of Sarah, as if in a different state of consciousness. Gavin came to Sarah's side and put his arms around her as they both looked in awe at the child in front of them. Tamara smiled and said, "Do you know what's going on, Sarah?"

In a faraway voice, Sarah replied, "Nature's baby needs nourishment here. I have done my part...and the baby will grow strong within the womb of nature."

Gavin had been granted this knowledge too as he turned Sarah towards him and pulled her tightly into his embrace. He whispered in her ear, "I love you."

The power of love was so strong within that circle in the woods, that the old woman felt for the first time in a long time that humankind, if only in part, would be saved, and her wrath upon the dominant species of her wonderful planet Earth will have dissipated.

Mother Nature would have let the asteroid hit the planet and start life on Earth again as things had stood up to Sarah becoming pregnant. Indeed, she didn't raise one finger to stop Atkinson Senior's plan, as she had all but given up on what she had come to consider an infestation upon her beautiful Earth.

Sarah's unborn baby looked straight into his mother's eyes and smiled as the mist returned around him. Sarah, still feeling quite at ease, smiled back. Turning to Gavin, she said, "Our job is complete." Sarah then looked at Tamara, while still smiling, saying, "I'm ready." She then looked back at the ancient beauty of Mother Nature, and bowing her head she said, "I entrust our baby into your care."

The floating mist that encapsulated the baby was now encompassing the old lady as well. As the gentlest of whirlwinds, it slowly twisted around her body. She lifted her arms to the sky, uttering a few incoherent words, and the mist into her form became absorbed. The old lady smiled and withdrew back into the forest. Tamara, Sarah and Gavin were left standing in the clearing.

Tamara placed both arms around her sister, and said, "Do you understand what has just taken place, my darling?"
Sarah smiled and nodded her head. She then noticed a small group of rabbits, munching on clover where the old woman had stood.
"Bunnies!" shouted Sarah, as she ran over to them and began stroking their ears.

Gavin glanced at Tamara with a concerned look in his eyes.
"Worry not, Gavin, everything is in order...she has just returned to the mindset that she held before she became pregnant."
"How can I return to mine?" he asked.
"That will be dealt with upon your re-entry to the Plane of Existence, and the memories of all who knew Sarah was pregnant will be altered. Your friends will no longer have any knowledge of it; your and Sarah's memories will be having conceived the child,

and delivering it to Nature on this very day. You now possess a pleasant memory of love, and the knowledge that you two have a child within the Realm of Nature – a child of utmost importance, that will one day be back in your lives...when the world needs him most," explained Tamara.

Gavin walked over to Sarah, took her hand, and pulled her to himself. "Come on, you, time to say goodbye to the bunnies. I think it's time we went home."

With that, Tamara depressed the button on her phone, and the opening in that enchanted forest was left with just a few rabbits chewing away on the lush green vegetation.

Gavin and Sarah found themselves parked at the roadside in their Jaguar.

"How do you feel, Sarah?"

"I feel great! We should do that again! That was the best love-making we have ever done!" she answered, with a flush in her cheeks.

"I must concur!" said Gavin with a satisfied smile on his face. The two embraced once more, and both had the sensation that they had just taken part in something monumental.

John Smith sat back in his chair with his feet on the desk. Dixie was sitting opposite him, scratching away at that night's list. Smith was mulling over all that had transpired since that night at Number 3 Lindale Mews, when he opened a 12 x 12" box made of skin. A smile curved his lips, as he remembered that very frightening night and the days that followed. The John Smith of now bore no resemblance to that frightened mouse of a man back then. For now, he was confident of his position, and his work was important – he was the Reaper. He was at ease with what he had to do, and he was good at what he did. He dispatched lives without a second's thought or care.

John looked over at Dixie and said, "How are you taking to your new work, Dixie?"

"I love it, Sir! It is still hard for me to believe that I am here doing what Tamara does!"

"Are you finding the work enjoyable, or is it difficult to do?" he enquired.

"I have taken to it like a duck to water, Sir," she replied.

"The thing that I don't understand is how you can step right in and begin writing the lists," he said.

"Well, the thing is, Sir, the list-making is the simplest part of Tamara's work. You see, the list is passed telepathically by Mr. Clarke while he is writing in the Great Book," informed Dixie.

"I see...so, you write my lists down through dictation, and then pass them to me," he said.

"It's not exactly that simple, Sir...I must cross-reference the names with their allotted mortality numbers. It would be impossible for Mr. Clarke to cross-reference all these names in his realm, because human names are just a part of his work. It makes sense that all the Listmakers do the searches for their own species in their own realm," she said.

"Well I must say, you are doing a splendid job, and I am enjoying working with you! Now, how's that soon-to-be husband of yours doing? I haven't seen him in a while," asked Smith.

"He is fine, Sir...I think he is getting bored being at home, but he certainly doesn't regret leaving the police force!"

"Have him come in and see me – he has more than earned his place in this company. I did tell him this when I saw him last."

"I will tell him. I'm sure he will be interested now. Being alone for long bouts of time is starting to wear thin with him...he is used to a more active life," said Dixie.

The Other Realm now looked quite different, as the two young Gods had put their stamp on it. They both had different ideas of how their area should look. Atkinson, who was now glad that the 'Junior' part of his name had gone forever, had brightened his father's domain considerably. He had progressive ideas that he intended to implement. His main aim was to stop the people of the world killing each other. His father had never cared for the human race – he could not stand its aggression – so over many thousands of years, he had grown to hate them. In the end, this proved to be his undoing.

The title of the 'Chosen One' wasn't sitting easily on his mind, as the Great Book had not told of why he was the Chosen One, nor did it inform him on how to lead.

Jeff Clarke was no longer a young reporter, for he also had been chosen for a different path. Without any knowledge of what was going on, he had been living and dying like Sarah, his many lives bringing him to this stage of his evolution. He now wielded the same power and had all the knowledge of his predecessor Dewhirst. He, however, wasn't alone as the Scribe had been, for he was gifted the company of his sweetheart Cindy.

Some rules of the Other Realm were changed by the new Alpha Reaper – one of them, in particular, being that no two Reapers could be on the Plane of Existence at the same time. That particular rule, enforced when Atkinson Senior had brought his son into the Reaper system, was the first to go. The Reapers and Scribe could join each other on the Plane of Existence, as well as the Other Realm. The Realm of Death would remain the same, only the Reaper in his Administration had sole use of that domain. Bringing back these rules made it so Atkinson, Smith or Clarke could move easily between realms.

Jeff Clarke sat at the Scribe's ornate desk, quill in hand, writing names in the Great Book. This book held the names of every life-form that walked, flew, swam, slithered or crawled on planet Earth throughout its long history. He had been deep in thought when Atkinson came into the room. Atkinson came up to Jeff, and placed a hand on his shoulder.

"With everything that has gone on since we took over this old place, I don't think I've ever really thanked you for what you did."

"I think my part was the easy part – Mr. Dewhirst did most of what I had to do. I don't think I could have taken Mr. Dewhirst's powers from him had he not wanted me to have them."

"This may be so – but you needed to be strong to consider even taking part in this."

"If I had felt as I do now, I would not have been worried," said Jeff.

"Indeed so, nevertheless, I could not have done this without you, and I am looking forward to working with you. My father and Dewhirst were the best of friends through many millennia. That friendship came to an end over my father's opinion of the human race. Dewhirst could see their potential; he knew they were not all greedy and self-opinionated. Because of this, they grew apart, and when there is a divide between Reaper and Scribe, that is where the trouble begins. I believe we both share the same opinion of the human race, and, therefore, will not suffer the same fate as my father and Dewhirst."

"One thing I have discovered since becoming the Scribe, and it's something that pleases me, is that it isn't just human names going into the Great Book," said Jeff.

"Oh yes – the belief that some humans have that only their species bears a soul – an arrogance known only to the human race, of course. Everything that lives and has a conscience must have a soul...indeed, how could it survive without one? Even the humans who preach that only they have a soul know only too well they are preaching a lie," said Atkinson.

"It has pleased me to find this to be true. But tell me this – why is it that we deal only with the humans? Because I scribe the names of everything onto the pages of this book," enquired Jeff.

"If you search your memories that belonged to Dewhirst, you will be able to understand this – but put quite simply, it's a matter of workload. We have different teams, and different Reaper systems for every different species on Earth. You, my friend, are the constant in all of this. John Smith and I work only with the humans – so as you write a name in the book, telepathically it's sent to the Listmaker who deals with that particular species. The Alpha Listmakers list human animals. There are many Reapers, and Listmakers, but we are the Alpha team, if you like. It's not because we are the best, it's because we deal with the dominant species," explained Atkinson.

This answer pleased Jeff, as it mirrored his feelings about animals having souls.

JOHN PAUL BERNETT

Chapter Two

The police station was not the happy place it once was. The thin blue line in that part of the world had seen more than its fair share of trouble since the start of the new millennium. The death of one of its long-standing police officers, Chief Inspector Jack Thompson, had rocked the morale of the whole station, quickly followed by many deaths during the first troubles at the turn of the century. The whole building itself had been razed to the ground, and a new one built in its place – then, the resignation of Chief Inspector Paul Johnson, without any warning, furthered the unrest. Yes...the police station was at a low point when the new Chief Inspector arrived for duty. As for the man chosen to bring harmony and stability back to this once well-run police station, there could not have been a worse choice.

Chief Inspector William Crawshaw was an arrogant, self-opinionated man. He had wormed his way up the promotion ladder by backstabbing and tale-telling. He would stop at nothing to get his foot on the next rung of the promotion ladder. He had undermined many good men and women who would have done the job far better than he. None of his past dealings to get him into the position he now held lay heavy on his conscience, because, quite simply, he didn't have one. He was not the right man for this job. It was that very thing that worried John Smith, and it was the reason he wanted to talk to Paul Johnson for quite some time.

In another part of town, Tom Harper was getting into his pristine white coat when Gavin jackson walked over to him.

"Good morning, Tom, how are you today?"

"I am exceedingly well this morning," he replied.

"Excellent, dear boy – did you go to Queen's Court last night?"

"We did! It was as fun as ever! We finished off over the road! John Smith has a few fans now, since his little escapade with that gang of ruffians," chuckled Tom.

Gavin laughed and said, "By the way – have you seen Sarah?"

"Oh God, please do not tell me she is somewhere in here, and you don't know where," said Tom, his happy mood deflating.

Gavin just shook his head and said, "When you find her, send her my way."

"You do realise if she is within earshot of us, I will be getting the third degree about last night? 'Have you kissed yet? Are you in love?' Et cetera, et cetera, et cetera."

Gavin just walked away laughing, leaving a very worried Tom Harper peering around the laboratory.

"Well, have you kissed yet?" said a voice from cooler number four.

"I do not converse with the dead – I am a scientist, not a medium," replied Tom.

The drawer burst open, and a covered body sat upright. Pulling the sheet from her head, Sarah said, "I am a small...but what has size got to do with whether you have finally kissed him or not?"

Tom just shook his head. "Whom I kiss or do not kiss is of no concern of yours, young lady – you are here to learn Mrs. Jackson, not to discuss my private affairs," instructed Tom.

"Then tell me if you did, and I will leave you alone until tea break...I promise!" pleaded Sarah.

"We have work to do. The rest of the people in these coolers are as they are supposed to be – dead, and are needing post-mortem preparation. Perhaps, you would be good enough to ready the examination table? And, if you're a very good girl, I will let you clean it after we have finished. Then you will be able to wash away all the blood and gore that your husband and I leave. Now, won't that make you a happy little Slabgirl?"

Sarah grinned and nodded her head.

"You are the strangest thing I've ever met...I have never met anyone more suited to a position than you are. Now go away, and leave me alone you horrible little person!" said Tom.

"Well, did you kiss him or not?" asked Sarah, her arms folded and hips cocked to one side as she looked straight at Tom's face.

"For the love of God! If it will shut you up, then yes, I kissed him! It was marvellous! It was the best kiss I've ever had! Now go away – for some deranged reason your husband wants to see you – and I want you to disappear! So go, and put a white coat on, now!"

Sarah leaped from the cooler drawer and ran off in the direction of Gavin's office and in a singing voice she yelled out, "Tomy loves John, they've finally kissed...yay!"

Tom Harper watched his giddy apprentice running towards his bosses' office and thought to himself, *what have I done?* He walked off, shaking his head. The memory of only two days before, when he last saw her and she was seven months pregnant had been eradicated from his mind. She was the same annoying person she had always been, and he had always loved...as much as Tom Harper could love a girl, that is.

Chief Inspector Crawshaw entered his new police station at ten-thirty, as he began his first day at his new placement. Walking past the Desk Sergeant, he said, "Coffee, milk, two sugars...and no calls this morning. Send me two men to move the stuff in my office."

"May I enquire who you are, Sir?" asked a befuddled Glenn Simpson.

"Who am I?!" shouted Chief Inspector Crawshaw.

"I'm not used to civilians walking in here, demanding beverages and furniture removal," said Sergeant Simpson.

"I am Chief Inspector William Crawshaw, sonny Jim!"

"Please address me by name or rank, Sir...as per regulations."

"If you enjoy wearing those stripes on your arm, learn to keep that clever tongue of yours still."

"I only have officers Harper and Bell available, Sir."

"Well send them up, you idiot," was the reply.

The Desk Sergeant called the two police officers over, and Linda Harper and Amanda Bell came to his desk. Upon seeing them, the new Chief Inspector was outraged. He came back to Sergeant Simpson and said, "I said, two men!"

"With respect, Sir, we do not have men and women...we have police officers, all of whom are capable of doing the same job, be that police work or office removal."

"Listen here, sonny, send the two girls out to help children cross the street, and bring me two policemen," demanded the outraged Chief Inspector as he turned and climbed the steps to his office.

The three police officers were left standing, looking at each other in total disbelief of what they had just witnessed.

"Do guys like that still exist?" asked Linda Harper.

"You two are police officers. Police officers hear abuse every day," replied Glenn Simpson.

"Yes, Sarge – but we don't expect it from our superior, in our own police station!" answered Amanda Bell.

"And you don't have to. I cannot tell you what to do either way, but if you take it further, I did witness the event. Now, do you want to help people cross the road while I get two men to do the work like the Chief Inspector asked me to...or do you want to do the work yourselves?" asked the Desk Sergeant.

The two police officers followed their superior up the steps and knocked on his door.

The front desk phone rang. "What is the meaning of this!?" growled the new Chief Inspector. "I distinctly asked for two men!"

"I know you did, Sir, but we both know you are not allowed to make such a sexist remark. And, begging your pardon, Sir, but what you said was sexist," reminded the Desk Sergeant.

"I will have your stripes for this!" shouted the angry Chief Inspector.

"Again, with respect Sir, no you won't. I have been a police officer for twenty-five years, and standing up for women officer's rights is not grounds for demotion," retorted Glenn Simpson.

"We shall see!" shouted the Chief as he slammed the phone down.

Looking at the two police officers in his office, he said, pointing at Linda Harper, "You – get me a cup of coffee! And you – bacon sandwich! And don't take all day about it!"

The two police officers left the office and marched down to the front desk where their sergeant was standing and said in unison, "We want to make a formal complaint!"

The Desk Sergeant gave them the relevant forms, and the new Chief Inspector didn't receive his sandwich or beverage.

In his office, Chief Inspector Crawshaw began to go through the drawers of his new desk, and found the bottom left-hand drawer to be locked. Having checked his bunch of keys, he discovered there was no key for the drawer, so he forcibly opened it. The drawer seemed to spring open, which he thought strange, but it was empty, so he pushed it back in. strangely, it sprang back open, as if something was stopping it from retracting. Upon closer inspection, the Chief Inspector saw something stuck in the back of the drawer. He put his arm into the drawer and took hold of what felt like a folder. After some gentle persuasion, the file yielded, and it was in Chief Inspector Crawshaw's hand. The contents of this presumably lost file – both the text and photographs – left him open-mouthed. He immediately phoned downstairs.

"Who are Atkinson, Atkinson, and Dewhirst?" he demanded.

The Desk Sergeant stuttered with his answer. "Um…uh…they were the old accountancy firm, Sir. Why do you ask?"

"Are they still around?"

"Yes, Sir – but it is run by different people now."

"I didn't ask who ran the company, I asked if it was still there!"

"Sorry Sir, yes, it is."

Chief Inspector Crawshaw slammed the phone down, removed his dark blue suit jacket from the back of his chair, put it on and left his office, holding his new acquisition. He walked straight past the front desk and out of the door.

At Atkinson, Smith & Clarke, Paul Johnson arrived to see John Smith. Mr. Braithwaite had shown him to the Reaper's office.

"Paul, my good fellow, how are you?"

"I'm good, thanks. Dixie keeps telling me you want to see me, so here I am!" said Johnson, casting a wink in Dixie's direction. She smiled and returned to her work.

"Yes, I did. How are you settling at home and how is the hiatus coming along?" queried Smith.

"Let's just say, you can have too much of a good thing. If I'm honest, John, I'm bored to my back teeth of sitting at home."

"I was hoping you were going to say that! How do you feel about taking your rightful place with us, here?"

"There isn't more trouble, is there?" said Johnson, looking worried.

"No, not as such, you just earned a place with us, and I am extending an invitation to join us," answered John.

"What will I do?"

"We will take care of that later. But don't worry, it won't be anything to do with accountancy," said Smith, with a little chuckle in his voice. The conversation was interrupted by a tapping on the door.

"There is a Chief Inspector Crawshaw here to see you, Sir," said Braithwaite. "Shall I have him make an appointment for the coming week?" the old gentleman continued.

John Smith glanced over at Paul Johnson with an inquisitive look in his eyes.

"Should I go?" asked Johnson.

"No, as you will be the person dealing with this kind of thing in the future, I would have you stay. Do show him in, Mr. Braithwaite."

"Very good, Sir," said the ancient employee.

Mr. Braithwaite ushered in Paul Johnson's replacement.

"Can I be of assistance, Chief Inspector?" asked John Smith.

"Well you can start by telling me what he is doing here!" said the arrogant Chief Inspector, pointing at Paul Johnson.

"Chief Inspector Crawshaw, I am used to my visitors having some manners when they address me, or at the very least, being polite. You, my good man, have neither virtue. If you want to talk with me, do so...however, I didn't realise I needed police permission to employ an ex officer," said Smith.

Chief Inspector Crawshaw, not used to being spoken to in this way, felt anger swell up within him.

"How dare you talk to me this way! Who do you think you are?" raged the Chief Inspector.

"I believe I am your host – and you are in my office – so kindly lower your voice and alter its tone. If you have official business with me, let's hear it. If not, this meeting is over, and good day to you, Sir!"

"This meeting is over when I say it's over!" roared the Chief Inspector.

"State your business," interjected Paul Johnson.

"You be quiet! I'm talking to the organ-grinder, not the monkey!"

Paul Johnson began to laugh. "You have been watching The Sweeney too much! Are you trying to intimidate us? Because if you are, you are a joke!" With that, Paul Johnson picked up his phone and rang the police station, then asked why the police were interrogating them. The answer was that there was no reason for the police to be there. Paul Johnson looked at John Smith and then turned to their guest, saying, "Chief Inspector Crawshaw is leaving."

John Smith opened the door and said, "Good day, Chief Inspector...do call again...but don't forget your manners next time."

"I will leave when I am ready!"

"You will leave now – or I will have you removed – and that won't go down well with your Superior, Detective Superintendent Malik, now, will it?" enforced Smith.

The new Chief Inspector left, promising he would return.

"What was that all about?" said Smith.

"I don't know...there's no reason he should come here; all the documentation about what happened, and everything entered into the computer no longer exists."

"We shall have to see. In the meantime, it looks like you've already begun your position here," said John Smith with a smile.

"I know this man. He must know something, and he will probably be back," said Johnson.

"Next time, we will be prepared for him. We can assume he's found something out – I wonder what it is?" said Smith.

"I'm sure we will soon know," answered Johnson.

"I had better make Atkinson aware of what has just occurred. I shall leave you in the hands of Dixie, if you will excuse me," said Smith, depressing the 'Atkinson' button on his phone.

"What do you want, Reaper?" said Atkinson, sounding like his father.

Smith looked shocked.

"Ha ha! Just kidding! How are you, John?" said Atkinson.

"You had me there for a minute," said John Smith.

"What do you think of the old place now that I've dragged it kicking and screaming into the 21stcentury?"

"It looks great! You have done well, I like it!" replied Smith.

"Ok, I guess you haven't come here to discuss my home furnishings. Do we have a problem?" asked Atkinson.

"We may have, Sire."

"Let me stop you there – we all still exist because of each other, so there are no superior beings anymore. I don't want to hear Sir, Sire, Great One or Milord. These are titles from my father's reign. We are all friends here," stated Atkinson.

John Smith smiled and said, "Thank you...but there may be a problem. We think the new Chief Inspector may be onto us."

"What makes you say this?" enquired Atkinson.

"He has just been to the office, and was quite rude. Luckily, I was speaking to Paul Johnson at the time, and he knew what to say."

"Is Paul onboard now?" asked Atkinson.

"Just today, I was talking to him about taking his place with us, when the new Chief Inspector came into the office."

"Excellent news! For now, leave the new Chief Inspector to me, and make sure Paul gets a phone."

"He already has one. I've been trying to get him to join us for some time, so I gave him one as a way of contacting me if he needed to," said Smith.

"Good thinking. I shall engage Jeff's, Tamara's, Dixie's, Sarah's, Gavin's and my buttons on it as well."

With that, the meeting was over, and John Smith returned to his office.

When Chief Inspector Crawshaw returned to the police station, he sped straight upstairs to his office. He took out the incriminating folder containing old documentation, which also held many photographs.

From the last days of 1999, the late Chief Inspector Jack Thompson had added to the file he started 25 years earlier. His eyes glistened as the new Chief Inspector pondered upon how he would use the strange contents of this seemingly plain manila folder to his advantage.

JOHN PAUL BERNETT

Chapter Three

It was a spectacular daybreak, with the first rays of sunlight bursting over the volcano on the horizon...but its magnificence could not match the mood of Chief Inspector Crawshaw's mind. He had been up all night and was still in his unchanged office. He, like everyone else, had heard the rumours of the first devastation and 'giant Warriors fighting' in this very city. He had, of course, dismissed this as the rampant lunacy of the small-minded people who lived there, but he was beginning to see things quite differently now. His twisted mind was already trying to think of how this could be used to his advantage. It wasn't the earlier notes of D.C.I. Thompson that interested him most...it was the later additions that intrigued him – especially the words 'Dewhirst – Scribe, Smith – Surrogate', and, best of all, 'Atkinson – Reaper', *was this real? Surely not!*

The world had almost ended at the turn of the century, and the epicentre of the devastation was right in the very city he was now stationed. *No – this couldn't be right, could it? And why would a young Chief Inspector with a good career in front of him, and an even better history, quite suddenly go and work for this accountancy firm?* There was no normal reasoning to any of this – and he was going to find out why. There were other names in that incriminating dossier, and one of them kept cropping up – Dr. Grayson's replacement, Gavin Jackson, the coroner.

The new Chief Inspector decided that he was to be the first on his list as he couldn't, for the moment, get anywhere near the accountancy firm.

The wonderful daybreak was being enjoyed by Paul Johnson and Dixie as well. This was the first time in existence that a Listmaker had a separate life away from the office. Paul Johnson, however, rather enjoyed having the elementals that came with the job. It meant that although his partner's working hours could sometimes be long, home life was stress-free with no chores. Yet, his mind was troubled. *Had something been overlooked*? The removed documentation and the fact he had covered his tracks was not helping...he knew of Detective Chief Inspector Crawshaw, and how he worked. He knew that if he could angle something to his advantage, he would. There would be no reason to have visited John Smith yesterday, unless he had discovered something.

At this point, Dixie brought him out of his thoughts and said, "What is so important that it has taken your mind off me?"

Johnson smiled and said, "Nothing, my love – I was miles away, that's all."

"If Chief Inspector Crawshaw is bothering you that much, we'd better have a word with Mr. Smith," said Dixie.

Paul just smiled and said, "I love you – but keep out of my head – it's a mixed up, crazy place."

Dixie laughed, and said, "Your head is the least-crazy place I know, and it seems too much to be a coincidence that you are finally working with us at the same time that this crass individual raises his ugly head."

"You could be right, Dixie...I think I will have an early start this morning. I am going to try and find out what our inquisitive Chief Inspector knows."

The clock in the clerk's office at Atkinson, Smith & Clarke struck 9 am when Paul Johnson entered.

"Good morning, Mr. Johnson, it is good to have you back with us," said Mr. Braithwaite as he handed Paul Johnson a dossier with the name 'Crawshaw' printed on a white label on its face.

With a confused expression, Paul Johnson, his head slightly to one side, gave a little smile to the old gentleman. Heading to John Smith's office he said, "Thank you...and good morning to you."

Upon entering the Reaper's office, John Smith said, "Good morning, Paul!" followed by Dixie saying, "Good morning!" as well.

"Didn't I just leave you in the shower?" mused Johnson.

Dixie just smiled, and said, "You will get used to your new way of travelling, darling."

"My new way of travelling?"

"Come and sit down, Paul...we have much to discuss," said John Smith.

Handing Paul a mobile phone, John said, "This is to replace the phone I gave you – it is now your main piece of equipment. It is, first of all, a communicator – you can now get in touch with any of us, including Mr. Atkinson and Mr. Clarke. If you depress the red button and then the name of whom you require, you will be transported to that person."

Holding his hand out to Paul Johnson, he said, "Again, welcome to the firm."

Paul Johnson looked at the phone in his hand, and then back at John Smith, and said, "May I use it as a phone?"

"Yes, when you don't use the red button, it can be used as a normal phone...but with a couple of advantages."

"Such as?"

"You never lose signal, and there are no network charges," said Smith with a smile.

"I like it already...now, down to business. If I am going to find out about our new Police Chief, I had better read this dossier on him."

"Indeed Paul, you must – but I think we can find you a more convivial place to do it in. Please come with me," said Smith, motioning towards the door.

They walked down the hall to the next office. John Smith opened the door and said with a chuckle in his voice, "This will be your office for the next...few thousand years."

Paul Johnson raised an eyebrow and surveyed his new office. It was decorated exactly to his liking, with a carved, ornate oak desk in the corner. The room had a music system with his entire record collection duplicated. Some of his favourite art adorned the walls, as did all of his certificates and awards he had picked up over the years as a police officer. One certificate on the wall intrigued him...it was a Private Investigator's license. He was intrigued – because he had never applied, nor thought about applying, for one. At this point, Mr. Braithwaite knocked on his door.

"Come in," said Johnson, placing a CD in the music station.

Mr. Braithwaite entered with a tray of tea and biscuits. "I have your favourite biscuits today, Sir," said the old gentlemen, gently placing the tray on his desk.

"That doesn't surprise me at all, Mr. Braithwaite," said Paul Johnson, quickly changing his mind from his favourite Custard Cream biscuits to Jammy Dodgers. He looked at the plate of biscuits and gave a little grin, as it now had four Jammy Dodgers resting upon it. "Thank you, Mr. Braithwaite."

"Will that be all, Sir?"

"For now, it will," replied Johnson.

Paul Johnson sat back in his deep buttoned leather chair, opened the file on the new Police Chief, took a bite of a Jammy Dodger and began to read.

It certainly didn't make for good reading. The file contained all of Chief Inspector Crawshaw's deeds as a police officer; not all of the information held within the folder could be said to be official. The information showed a trail of deceit, bullying, homophobia, prejudice towards women, and any race of people whom he thought was beneath him. The file also showed he was a master at covering his tracks, with an obvious ability to deceive people. In fact, what this file showed was that he owned none of the skills that would make a good police officer – and all of the skills that would make a good criminal.

Taking the final piece of the last Jammy Dodger and popping it into his mouth, he rose from his chair and made his way back to the Reaper's office with the document under his arm. Once inside, he put the folder on the Reaper's desk.

"Have you seen this, John?"

"Yes...I saw it just after Braithwaite had it printed; it doesn't make for comfortable reading, does it?"

"Indeed, it does not," was Johnson's reply.

"Now that you have his background, you had better read this one. I'm afraid it's even worse."

"I don't see how that is possible, but I will take a look."

Johnson's mouth opened as he lifted his eyes back to John Smith. "Is this a copy of the folder that Crawshaw has?"

"The very one," answered Smith.

"My God! The last entry was on the day my old Chief Inspector died! How had he obtained so much information about Atkinson, Dewhirst and the current Atkinson?"

"That is neither here nor there – we are all implicated in this, and, therefore, must do something about it. You may have noticed the copies of the deeds for this place, the Mews, and all the other property and land, showing how long they have been in our possession. With all this information, he could go to the press...or even worse, he could begin an investigation into what we do here, and that will not go down well with Atkinson, I can tell you that, my friend!"

"You're the Grim Reaper, for God's sake! Can't you just...take him out, or something?"

"I can't 'Take him out', as you say, until his time is up and he is on my list," said a frustrated John Smith.

"Atkinson Junior did when he first came back – he was killing people left, right and centre!"

"He was working to a set plan as predicted in the old book, and not a plan for a cover-up...which is what we must do now," answered Smith.

"I will go through this in detail, and come up with an idea of where to go with it. There is an answer to every problem...my old Chief Inspector told me that."

"You are going to be an asset to this old company, Paul..." was John Smith's last gambit to the conversation as he added, "The Realm of Death awaits, and I cannot be the one who is late."

With that, the Reaper picked up his scroll from Dixie, and left via the great door behind his desk.

Paul Johnson looked over at Dixie and said, "Was that a grim joke? It looks like I'm going to be busy for a while."

Dixie got up from her desk and moved over to where Johnson was standing. She put her arms around his neck, saying, "I know you are, my love... if I can help in any way, I will. I don't think joke-telling is Mr. Smith's forte."

She gave him a kiss and walked back to her desk. With the folders of incriminating evidence firmly under his arm, he returned to his office, sporting a worried look.

In the Other Realm, Atkinson was alone with his thoughts. He was privy to what had just gone on in the Reaper's office. He understood Johnson's simple solution, but knew only too well what the outcome of such a move would be. *If something could happen to Crawshaw that didn't involve the offices of Atkinson, Smith & Clarke to terminate his existence, that would be a reasonable conclusion to this bad situation...*so, he would keep his options open.

He wondered how his father would have handled this and then stopped himself, because Life and Death were going to carry on, as they were supposed to, without interference from his realm. He decided to visit Paul Johnson in his office.

Johnson was looking through the folder when Atkinson appeared.

"I like your office, Paul," said Atkinson.
"The new rules are working, I see," replied Johnson.
"New rules?"
"You are here, John Smith is in the next room...and we're not sitting in the middle of a storm."
"I see – yes, the new rules are working fine. Are you settling in okay?"
"I am, thanks...but it's a bit daunting when the main boss just appears in your office. Does anyone else know you're here?" queried Johnson.
"No, and that's how it stays for the moment. John Smith is right – we cannot change a human's life number. It would cause far too much paperwork for my partner Mr. Clarke. On the other hand, we cannot afford to have this troublesome policeman meddling in our affairs."
"I take it that's why you have come to see me? Do you want me to kill him?"
"Calm down, dear boy – you killing him would be the same as us killing him. I have come to you because I am going to use Smith's Listmaker to entrap him."
"In what way? Remember, she's not just one of your minions anymore, she's about to become my wife."
"In the old ways, you are all my minions to do with as I please, but I've changed those ways, remember?"
"Yes...sorry. What do you have in mind?"

In the adjacent office, John Smith had returned from the Realm of Death, and instantly, his senses were off the scale. He looked over at Dixie and said, "Prepare yourself, Dixie – you are about to have an audience with Atkinson."

Dixie immediately left her desk to prepare.

Johnson looked intently at Atkinson, waiting for his answer, and added, "What can Dixie do to eliminate your adversary?"

"My adversary? If only he were the one I had to worry about...this pathetic little human is not our worry, he is an inconvenience and nothing more. He is human, and therefore not a problem. Now that I have stepped on the Plane of Existence, I am sensing a bigger danger. Tell me, has the Jackson male child arrived?"

"I didn't know they were expecting a child," said Johnson.

"That means the child is already with Nature. We have no time to lose, and this new Chief Inspector is a decoy. I must talk with Smith's Listmaker."

With that, Atkinson disappeared and reappeared in the Reaper's office.

"I was expecting you," said Smith, bowing his head.

"Where is your Listmaker?" asked Atkinson.

"I am here, at your service, Milord," said Dixie, kneeling before him.

"I thought my instructions were no kneeling, and no 'Lording'!"

"Thousands of years of devotion to the Ancient Gods will not disappear overnight," observed Smith.

"Yes, I take your point. Listmaker, please stand, we have much to discuss."

"I shall offer my office as I have things to take care of," said Smith, leaving the room.

John Smith knocked on the door of the office adjacent to his and walked in.

"What is going on, John?" asked Paul.

"Relax Paul, you have to realise, the girl you are to marry isn't human and has supernatural duties to perform. One of those duties will be with our new Chief Inspector."

"I don't know if I like the sound of this," said Johnson.

"Dixie has two lives – a type of human existence with your good self, and as one of Atkinson's otherworldly Warriors. You have seen her in warrior mode, and she bears no resemblance to the little lady you will marry. The human Dixie is the girl gifted to you for your work in helping Atkinson defeat his father; she will be true and loyal, and everything you want her to be. My Listmaker is an entity unto herself, and will follow Atkinson's orders to the letter. You will have no knowledge or say in her activities in the Other Realm," instructed Smith.

"I think I see what you mean," said Johnson.

"Atkinson thinks Chief Inspector Crawshaw is a decoy; I have also had thoughts in this vein...something much bigger is happening," said Smith.

"I think it has something to do with Gavin and Sarah," added Johnson.

"Yes, their child is about to be born, and the outcome will have repercussions for all of existence," informed Smith.

"I wasn't even aware she was pregnant until Atkinson told me," said Johnson.

"That is not entirely accurate; you did know, but because of the nature of what was about to happen, anyone with knowledge of the pregnancy had their memories cleared of the baby's existence."

"I am never going to understand this company," said Johnson.

"Now you are part of us, you will Paul – believe me, you will."

Next door, Dixie was now stood upright, and Atkinson had put her at ease.

"I want you to work on this new Chief Inspector, Listmaker. It would be easy to get Tamara to do it, but this is your time, so it must be you. It will be like teamwork, because I want you to remove all the evidence he has acquired once he begins to start using it. Then, your husband-to-be can prove to his old employers their new Chief is not the right man for the job."

"I won't let you down," said Dixie.

"Failure is not an option in this case; there is something out there waiting for the birth of the child. Should this child be found, whoever controls the infant will control all of existence – which will include all that we do, too. I have not gone through all that I went through to have something else governing what I do," said Atkinson.

"I will start right away," said Dixie.

"Do you have a plan?"

"If I can help fight off sea monsters, then I can deal with a troublesome police officer," said Dixie with confidence.

"I will entrust this matter into your capable hands," answered Atkinson, as he returned to the Other Realm to inform the Scribe as to what was about to take place.

Dixie knew this was her time to impress Atkinson, and she would not let anything stop that from happening.

Chapter Four

Tamara was in a daydream, with absolutely nothing to do but relax, when she was brought back to the present with a start. She was experiencing an unusual feeling she had never felt before. It was neither fear nor problematic, it was just a feeling that she should be somewhere else. At that precise moment, Sarah and Gavin appeared.

"What is going on?" asked Sarah.
"I wasn't entirely sure until you two lovely people appeared. Now that you are here, I think we are needed elsewhere," announced Tamara.

She held out both hands; Gavin took one, and Sarah took the other. Instantly all three beings disappeared, reappearing in the Realm of Nature.

The whole area was vivid green with foliage. Bluebells carpeted the floor, and the sky was awash with all manner of blue. Standing in front of them, surrounded by all kinds of creatures from all over her realm, mingling with animals from the past – long since extinct – stood Mother Nature. To the amazement of the open-mouthed Sarah, there were also animals that were supposed to be mythical...but as the silver-white mane of Juliantrium, the winged unicorn, was nestling on her shoulder, mythical was not a word she could use anymore.

"The time is nigh, little one," said Tamara.

Sarah's gaze moved from the unicorn to Mother Nature, who now lay upon a bed of feathers. The animals moved aside, as if to make a pathway for Sarah to walk to Nature herself. Sarah's hands lifted as several fairies, dressed in their finest garments, guided her, all of them smiling as they took her hands. She felt pain in her lower abdomen, and looked back at Tamara and Gavin. Her sister smiled and said, "Everything will be fine, you'll see."

Sarah looked straight into Gavin's eyes and mouthed, 'I love you'. Gavin shouted back, "I love you, too!" He then looked at Tamara with questioning eyes.

Everything is fine, Gavin; you are about to witness something that has never happened before...the birth of a being so powerful that two mothers had to carry him, she told Gavin telepathically.

Gavin thought back to his first meeting with Slabgirl, and the whirlwind romance that had led to this day.

It wasn't a whirlwind, Gavin. Many thousands of years ago, the Gods created the Sentinel's lineage for the sole purpose of delivering you here, today. Sarah's journey to here was laid out by the Gods...yours, by Atkinson himself, said Tamara in a mental whisper.

As the fairies brought Sarah closer to Mother Nature, the pains grew worse, and she began to scream out loud in agony. A wave of fairy-folk flew in from the trees, and lifted Sarah's legs off the ground, carrying her into the arms of Mother Nature. As soon as she was in Nature's embrace, four centaurs trotted into a guard position. Protection was given to the front, back, and both flanks of Mother Nature and Sarah. Each centaur stood looking outward, furrowing the ground with their right front hooves, like a bull. The four centaurs drew back an arrow, and rested them onto their bows, all four pointing outwards.

A ring of a thousand fairies astride dragonflies hovered above, offering protection from the sky. Over the fairies, the sky had turned to a myriad rainbow. At this point, all the animals began to kneel down; Sarah's muffled screams were obliterated by the buzz of dragonfly wings, signalling that she was now totally at one with Nature. It was as if the two beings were morphing into one. A cocoon enveloped both females as Sarah's screams diminished, and Nature's true voice sang out into the heavens.

They both disappeared within the cocoon, and everything grew silent. For one magic moment, all the animals, all the insects, the Listmaker and Sentinel were still and in total silence.

The midday sun disappeared as the moon totally eclipsed its brilliance. The silence was deafening, but as soon as the moon began to move past the Sun, the silence broke to the loudest scream yet. As both Nature and Sarah together bore down, the Child of Nature began to breathe air for the first time. Inside the cocoon, movement could be seen, as it began to change colour. Tiny cracks began to appear in its beautifully-designed outer skin, and brilliant beams of light thrust outward into the heavens, announcing the arrival of the long-awaited Saviour of Humanity.

The sides of the cocoon broke away and fell to the ground, revealing nature's child. Woodland sparrows carrying spider webs flew around the infant, twisting in and out, weaving a fine cloth of silk around the child. Mother Nature held her hands in the air and beckoned everyone to come and take a look. She was sitting down, quite naked. Resting on her breast was Sarah, unconscious and also naked, and in Sarah's arms a child. a man-child of such beauty, with green cat like-eyes and the sweetest smile. The creatures of the forest bowed down when they gazed upon his face. Tamara leaned over and whispered in Gavin's ear, "You are the father of the greatest being to live on this Earth. He will bring peace and tranquillity back to this land. He is the Earth's last hope, and you sired him."

"What happens now?" asked Gavin.

"When Sarah wakes she will kiss him, and hand him to one of the centaurs, who will keep him for the first most crucial moments of his life, during which time the fairy-folk will lend a hand. Then, he will spend time with Mother Nature. Through thought, you and Sarah will know everything he is doing, and he will feed off you both as you go on about your ordinary – and – supernatural, lives."

"Our supernatural lives? I thought we had done our part. I thought we only had to deal with a troublesome police officer," said Gavin.

"So, you know about him?" asked Tamara.

"Not as such, it's just a feeling," replied Gavin.

"Now Nature's child is here, there will be many who will try and stop his development Which, my friend, is why you and Sarah, John Smith, Dixie, Paul Johnson and Mr. Clarke are here."

"But I thought it was for the Atkinson fight."

"No, Gavin – all that has happened was predicted in the Great Book – and the arrival of the Nature Child, although a couple of years late, is the reason for our new band of Warriors...to protect the child to our deaths."

The conversation was interrupted by the four centaurs marching past, the third one carrying the baby. As they looked over, Mother Nature was adorning Sarah in a dress made of ladybird wings that had been sewn together with thread spun by the nimble fingers of ancient elves. The garment placed on Sarah's body was a perfect fit; she felt an overwhelming feeling of euphoria, and power. Mother Nature kissed her and placed her hand on Sarah's head, saying, "His heart is your heart, your love and strength is his, and this will forever be. For the time being, I give you back to the Sentinel known as Gavin Jackson. Know that you are the mother of the Saviour of all existence, but for now, return to Sarah – the wife of the Earth-Child Gavin Jackson."

Sarah's eyes opened, and she rubbed them, drying her tears, smiling at the vision of beauty in front of her.

Sarah then turned and ran to meet Gavin, saying, "I'm starving! Can we eat?"

Gavin, who found himself in his office, not quite understanding what just happened, enquired, "What happened to Tamara?"

Tamara instantly arrived, saying, "I will have to have that phone of yours fixed, it keeps calling me!"

Sarah ran into Tamara's arms and said, "Now that you are here will you come and have dinner with us?"

A voice from outside the office shouted "Lunch."

JOHN PAUL BERNETT

Chapter Five

hief Inspector Crawshaw was sitting in his office, his feet resting on a pile of unfinished paperwork on his desk, when the internal phone began to ring.

"What do you want?" answered the Chief Inspector.

"There is a woman at the front desk to see you, Sir," said the Desk Sergeant.

"Who is she, and what's her business?"

"She works for Atkinson, Smith & Clarke, and says she has information in which you might be interested," was the answer.

"Bring her to my office," he said, replacing the receiver.

He grinned and removed his feet from his desk.

There was a knock on the door, followed by a police officer escorting the young woman. Chief Inspector Crawshaw looked her up and down, his eyes fixating on her ample cleavage.

"Come in...take a seat, Miss...uh..."

"You can call me Dixie."

"We have already met, Dixie...although introductions didn't take place. Now, how can I be of assistance?" said the Chief Inspector, taking his gaze away from her breasts just long enough to dismiss the police officer standing at the door. "Shut the door behind you – and arrange for coffee or something to be brought up. Now Dixie, where were we?"

"You said we have already met. – and yes, we have – when you came to see Mr. Smith. I am a secretary at Atkinson, Smith & Clarke, and I have some information you might find interesting."

"What kind of information?"

"I feel strange being inside a police station...I would feel more comfortable somewhere else. The more comfortable I am, the more information I might give. What do you guys do in this part of town for lunch?" asked Dixie.

"In that case, never mind the coffee – I will take you to a place more convivial, and we can talk there while we eat," he said, his lips now curling into a smile.

Dixie crossed her legs, and her short skirt revealed a bit more thigh, which tore the Chief Inspector's gaze from her breasts as she said, "Yes, that would be lovely, Chief Inspector! I do so like men with power!"

Chief Inspector Crawshaw was on his feet in a flash, and police work became even lower on his agenda than usual, as he said, "I will show you to my car."

"That sounds delightful, Chief Inspector!" answered Dixie.

As he led Dixie past the front desk, he said, "Hold all my calls – no matter who they are!"

"But what if..."

"Shut up you fool, I said no calls! Now, get on with whatever it is you're supposed to be doing!" retorted Chief Inspector Crawshaw.

Sergeant Glenn Simpson just looked at him, and jotted something down in his notebook.

As the Chief Inspector and Dixie left the police station and drove off in his car, a shadowy figure was standing in the bushes near the doorway. It stepped out into the sunlight and began to move into the police station. It took the form of Crawshaw, and walked past the front desk. The Desk Sergeant still couldn't believe how he had been spoken to not a minute before.

They both looked at each other, and Glenn Simpson put his head down and continued to write in the notepad on his desk. The imposter climbed the stairs, and entered the Chief Inspector's office.

Once inside, it began to rummage through the drawers of the filing cabinet, and then the desk. Upon reaching the bottom drawer, it pulled out the file and flipped through the pages. Realising it had procured the information it had come for, it merged itself into the wall to await the Chief Inspector's return.

At the mortuary, Gavin and Sarah had arrived back after their lunch with Tamara.

"Just in time, the little gory pest is back! I have a wonderful job for you...but first, put on your white coat because there's blood involved," said Tom to Sarah.

Sarah jumped with delight and ran off to the changing room.

"Now we are alone, I need to have a word with you, Gavin," said Tom Harper.

"You'll have to be quick – you mentioned blood – she'll be in that coat and back out here in a flash!" said Gavin.

"No, she won't, I've hidden her white coat, and it will take her a while to find it."

Gavin just smiled and said, "What's on your mind, Tom?"

"We had a visitor this morning. I say 'visitor', but it was more of a...a..."

"Come on, Tom, spit it out!"

"All I can describe it as is a strange occurrence inside your office," said Tom.

"Tom, we are men of science, what are you trying to say?"

"Yes, my mind is a scientific one...but I saw doors and drawers opening and closing...the perpetrator seemed to be a...dark shadow moving around," answered Tom.

Gavin looked shocked, and said, "I will have it looked into."

"So you don't think I'm going mad?" asked Tom.

"You sir, are the sanest person I know, but I think we'd better keep this between ourselves, if you know what I mean," said Gavin.

"If I see it again, I will alert you to its presence," said Tom, feeling more at ease now that he had informed Gavin.

Gavin began to smile and motioned Tom towards the changing room door, where Sarah emerged. Turning around, Tom said, "You look ridiculous! Take that off at once!"

Sarah, not being able to find her white coat, had taken one of Tom's, the bottom of which was dragging the floor. The arms were twelve inches past her hands, but rolled up just beyond her wrists. Both Gavin and Tom giggled. Sarah stamped her foot on the ground and did that very thing, impishly removing the garment.

Both men shouted simultaneously, "Sarah!" As she picked the garment up from the floor, she turned and took her naked self back to the changing room. Gavin and Tom just looked at each other. Gavin raised his hands into the air and turned in the direction of his office, walking away and giggling to himself. Tom just stood there with a red face.

"Your white coat is in the tea cabinet!" shouted the embarrassed lab tech.

Sarah came back into the room properly attired, and said, "What was it doing in there?"

"I don't know why it was in there! Why were you naked under that coat?"

"I'm always naked under my coat when I'm working with body parts. I don't want stains all over my underwear now, do I, Tommy?"

"My name is Tom! And that was a bit too much information, thank you very much, young lady!"

"You asked me! But to tell the truth, though, the rough cloth doesn't half chafe your nipples!"

"Sarah!! Just because you now know I'm gay, it doesn't mean you have to feel comfortable talking about your intimate areas...you give me enough nightmares as it is!"

Sarah giggled and said, "I've made you blush!"

"No, you haven't! Now make some coffee."

"Coffee, and not tea?! Haha! I have put you in shock as well! What about this blood?"

"Coffee first, then blood – now go away, you vile creature."

Gavin was now in his office, looking to see if anything was missing. After a thorough search, all seemed to check out, and nothing was absent. Later, he phoned John Smith.

"Hello, Gavin, how are you?" said the Reaper.

"Do you believe in ghosts?" Gavin asked.

"A strange question to be asking me...I make ghosts!" he quipped.

"I am serious."

"In that case, no I don't, not in the Dickensian meaning of the word, that is. But people do sometimes get 'glimpses' of beings on a different plane. Why do you ask?"

"How would they look?" asked Gavin.

"This is a strange line of questioning, Gavin, I'll be right over."

John Smith materialised in the seat opposite Gavin Jackson.

"Now, what is this all about, Gavin?" continued the Reaper.

"Tom Harper, my assistant."

"Yes, I know Tom quite well."

"So I've heard," said Gavin, a smile coming to his face.

"Of course, not as well as I hope to..." said Smith with a knowing smile.

"About that – you two might need to come out pretty soon, as someone we both know and love has found out," said Gavin.

41

"Ahh, did Slabgirl wear Tom down?"

"Got it in one!" answered Gavin.

John just laughed and said, "It was dark in that closet, so maybe it's for the best. But that isn't why I'm here, is it…what's the problem?"

"A shadow…lurking about in here and going through my cupboards and drawers."

"That is not a ghost," answered Smith.

"Well, in that case, what is it?"

"What people describe as 'ghosts', as I've already said, are beings in another realm. Some of them are between this life and the next one. On the Plane of Existence, you die, and if you have not caused danger to yourself or other humans, your soul is instantly reborn to a newborn human. That is, of course, the route for most humans. If you haven't cared for Nature or humankind, you become part of the Earth – as in an elemental. You then spend the rest of your existence in toil. If you have actively worked against Nature, then you simply become part of the food chain, and your soul goes into a holding place for safe-keeping. It then goes to the next dominant species that take over the humans, when Nature has had enough of the present dominant species."

"What about when people see relatives, like old grandmas, parents and children that have never done anything wrong?" asked Gavin.

"What you have there is the mind working. If you see one of these elementals in another realm, not long after a relative has died, your mind simply puts that face to the elemental," said Smith.

"Okay then – so what did Tom see?"

"Here is where it gets a bit strange," said John.

"Here it gets strange?" gasped Gavin.

"Yes. In the Other Realm, time is different, and there can be a gap between the soul leaving one body and arriving at the next. It's because the Scribe…"

"Jeff?" said Gavin.

"Yes, Jeff; sometimes he needs time for the paperwork, so in that realm, time can be distorted to suit his needs. The human soul then simply lives in that realm until time catches up with it, which it invariably does."

"Okay, but what about ghosts?" said Gavin.

"Certain people can occasionally see into the Other Realm. When this happens, they see the souls between Death and Life. They aren't 'ghosts', and they do not exist on the Plane of Existence. As I've already said, these people every now and again see into the Other Realm."

"So, what was in my office this morning?"

"I don't know – but I will find out," said the Reaper.

In a pub on the outskirts of town, Chief Inspector Crawshaw was wining and dining Dixie.

"It is one of my rules never to mix business with pleasure, but rules are meant to be broken – don't you agree, Dixie?"

"I live my life breaking rules."

"It's a wonder our paths haven't crossed before, in that case."

"Oh, I'm too smart to be caught, Chief Inspector."

"I like your style, Dixie."

"I think you like more than my style, Chief Inspector."

"I don't think your boyfriend would like us having this conversation."

"What has my boyfriend, as you call him, got to do with this?" asked Dixie, putting her elbows on the table, allowing the Chief Inspector a clear view down her cleavage.

"Not a thing," said Crawshaw.

"You took his job – why stop there?" quipped Dixie.

In a dark corner, watching this seduction unfold, stood Atkinson. He grinned, and was very impressed with Tamara's understudy, as he returned to his realm to report the day's events to his partner.

Upon his return, Atkinson went straight to Jeff Clarke. To his surprise, the Scribe looked...different; not older, but he didn't look like a kid anymore.

"Is everything sorted out?" said Jeff.

"Yes...things have been sorted, but..."

"Who is the Dark One, and is he a problem?" interrupted the Scribe.

"You know he's here, then?"

"Yes, I do...is the child protected?" asked Clarke.

"He has been born and is with the Centaurs."

"Excellent. I have a question for you, though, Atkinson."

"What is that, my friend?"

"How do I know all this?" said Jeff as he placed his quill on his desk and turned to face Atkinson.

"I've been waiting for this...in fact, I have needed this to happen."

"What has happened?"

"You have quickened – and may I say, welcome back!"

"Who are you welcoming back?" asked Jeff.

"I gratefully welcome the emergence of your good self, now totally joined with the mind of Dewhirst."

"It will be a good merger, but my place is now forever in this domain; I only accept this merger on that basis. The reaping will now be performed by you and Smith only."

"Agreed, old friend."

Jeff Clarke began to tremble, and then shake. His arms were thrown outwards, and light began to pulsate from his body. "What is happening!?" screamed Jeff.

"Be still, and just accept me," said a familiar voice in Jeff's head.

Jeff lifted slowly off the ground, twirling in a counter-clockwise direction. A vortex began to form around the young man as he rose higher, and spun faster. With lightning flashing all around him, he shouted again, "What is happening?!"

Atkinson looked up, and in a quiet voice, said, "Thank you, Jeff. We couldn't have done this without your help."

Although Jeff was spinning now at great velocity, a tunnel of calm opened up before him, and inside the tunnel stood Cindy with her arms outstretched. Jeff walked towards her, and as they came together, in each other's arms, the gas main under the newspaper building blew up – sending them, and the rest of the people within the building – to oblivion, as John Smith finally cut the mortal cords of Jeff and Cindy.

The spinning vortex slowed down and returned to the ground. The flashing lightning stopped and the dust settled, and standing there was the regenerated Dewhirst in full body armour, with his waist-long black hair, and a sparkle back in his eyes. And so it was that the figurehead signpost at the offices on the Plane of Existence changed to 'Atkinson, Dewhirst & Smith'. A rejuvenated Atkinson and Dewhirst were now back in command, albeit with a different, but just as powerful, Atkinson.

In the Maternity Ward of a nearby hospital, two new mothers were holding two new babies – one of them a girl and the other a boy... a boy destined for greatness in the future and a girl who would love him unconditionally.

JOHN PAUL BERNETT

Chapter Six

ohn Smith, Tamara, Sarah, Gavin, Dixie and Paul Johnson all stopped what they were doing, as a sudden rush of immense power surged through their bodies, and instantaneously all their phones rang. The name 'Dewhirst' had replaced 'Clarke'. Instinctively, everyone knew what had just occurred, and went back to their business, as all knowledge of Jeff Clarke had disappeared from their collective memories.

Lunch was over, and Chief Inspector Crawshaw was driving Dixie back to the police station. His hand crept onto her knee, and she offered no resistance.

"Well, Dixie, should we go back to the police station?"

"Work can wait...who wants to talk about accountancy and stuffy old police work? I can think of much better things to do," smiled Dixie.

"In that case, your place, or mine?" said Chief Inspector Crawshaw.

"Yours, darling, we don't want to be disturbed now, do we?"

The car suddenly sped up as the eager Chief Inspector put his foot down hard on the accelerator.

"So, what was it you wanted to talk to me about?"

"For now, let's not talk about work, because you wouldn't believe what goes on there," said Dixie.

"What would you say if I told you I already knew?" said the arrogant Chief.

"Believe me, Chief Inspector, you don't," answered Dixie. "I have worked there for years, and I don't know all that goes on there – but I know enough to interest you," she continued.

"In that case, if you are good to me, I will show you something that will blow your mind...if you are a very good girl."

"I can be the best girl you have ever had if you are worth it," answered Dixie.

Chief Inspector Crawshaw knew by later that afternoon there would be another notch added to his bedpost. He smiled smugly, as his conceited mind looked forward to an afternoon of lust with the idiot girl at his side.

Back in the Other Realm, the young Dewhirst was a magnificent sight to behold. He stood almost nine feet tall; slim with a muscular build. His long, raven-black hair fell all the way down his back, and not a hair was out of place. His body armour shone like new. From his features, you could tell it was Dewhirst – but only just. This God of Death now had all the ancient knowledge combined with a young, strong body – and it felt good. He walked over to Atkinson, and extended his hand in friendship. Atkinson duly obliged.

"How do you feel?" asked Atkinson.

"Rejuvenated!" answered Dewhirst.

"Your dwelling is ready for you; also, you can come and go as you please now, there is no restriction on how many of us can be in the same domain at the same time," instructed Atkinson.

"That does sound wonderful as an idea, but what are the consequences?" asked Dewhirst.

"I don't foresee any that can't be overcome," answered Atkinson.

"We shall see; this time, though, as I've said, I don't want to reap. I want to observe the humans, to see if they are indeed worth saving."

Dewhirst then turned and walked towards his great desk, picked up his quill, and started writing names in the old book.

He was back, doing the job created for him alone – and happy to be there.

The drive came to an end as the Chief Inspector's car pulled into his driveway. He exited and walked towards the front door. Dixie raised an eyebrow in disgust at this animal's manners and helped herself out of the car. She then followed him up to his front door. He unlocked the door and walked inside, allowing it to fall back towards Dixie, who had to stop it with her hand. The thought of tearing this insignificant human in half was hard to keep as a thought, but she knew she couldn't harm the pathetic worm.

"Come in, make yourself comfortable. Would you like a drink, or should we get straight on with it?"

"I thought we weren't going to talk about work," said Dixie.

"I'm not," said Crawshaw.

Incredible...what an asshole, she thought to herself. Looking at him, she said, "What have you in mind?"

"The bedroom is through there," he said, pointing at the bedroom door.

Dixie smiled and walked in the direction of the bedroom. Looking over her shoulder at Crawshaw, she said, "You'd better be good, because if you are one of these 'quickie' types, I may have to rip your head off and eat it. You know what we accountants are like, my darling..."

Chief Inspector Crawshaw gulped; he knew she was just joking, but he had seen photographs of people with their heads torn from their bodies, and in this very city!

"Umm...this is all moving a bit too fast, let us just get to know each other a little bit better first," said a less-confident Chief Inspector.

Dixie just smiled and said, "That works for me, shall we go back to your office, and put our minds together instead of our lust?"

"Yes, let's do that."

Dixie's knees escaped the groping fingers of the Chief Inspector on the journey back to the police station. At their arrival, the Chief Inspector walked straight past the front desk without looking at anybody.

"Are you okay, Sir?" asked Sergeant Glenn Simpson, being slightly confused, as he thought the Chief Inspector had already returned to his office just after leaving.

He just walked on by, taking no notice, and Dixie gave the Sergeant a wink. The Desk Sergeant smiled.

Once inside the office, Crawshaw was not his usual bombastic self; this girl had frightened him, and his male-supremacist stance had taken a knock. *Was it frivolity, or was she serious about her actions...*thought the Detective Chief Inspector. He was hoping the police station gave him some sanctuary, should she be one of the monsters that presided over the old accountancy firm.

"Shall I show you mine – or do you want to show me yours, Chief Inspector?" asked Dixie, her lips curling into a grin.

"Well, we don't have much time, for I am a busy man. So, what did you want to tell me?" stuttered the Chief Inspector.

"Do you know what commodities our accountancy firm deals with?"

"I know that it isn't money," he answered.

"Well done, Chief Inspector."

"Out with it...as I said, I'm a busy man."

"You'll find it hard to believe, what I'm about to tell you."

"You're only a mere secretary – I will tell you what I know and that I am probably more in the know than you are!"

"I don't think so, Chief Inspector," said Dixie as she stood, then moved over to the window, allowing the bright sunlight to shine through her dress, showing off the outline of her curves.

He turned to view the show and stated, "You work for the Grim Reaper!"

"A little theatrical my dear, but yes, I suppose I do. So, what else do you know?" asked Dixie, as she parted her legs slightly, allowing the sun to outline the inside tops of her thighs.

"That your Mr. Atkinson was responsible for a lot of unsolved murders that your boyfriend couldn't pin on him!"

"You do know your stuff, Chief Inspector! But let's be serious – you cannot arrest our Mr. Smith for being the 'Grim Reaper', now, can you? Just imagine the paperwork! And, it is also hard to arrest a killer who is already dead. Now, Chief Inspector, what if my files placed me as a witness to everything that occurred during the murders at the end of the last century? You could be the man who closed the case!"

The Chief lifted his gaze from Dixie's transparent backlit dress and said, "You have such a file?"

"I do," said Dixie.

"I could solve all the murders?"

"Indeed you could, Chief Inspector."

"Where is this file?"

"It's in my safe-keeping, and, at your disposal – if you are a good boy."

"When can I see this file?"

"I will be in touch, Chief Inspector," said Dixie, as she picked her handbag up from the desk and walked towards the door.

Chief Inspector Crawshaw drooled whilst he watched every movement of her bottom as she crossed the floor and then left the room.

Leaving the police station, Dixie depressed the 'A' button on her phone and was instantly transported to Atkinson.

"What do you have to report?" asked Atkinson.

Dixie, who was kneeling, said, "The game is afoot, Milord."

"Good work, Dixie. Did you sense anything worrying about Crawshaw?"

"No, Sire, but there was something else in the room...something listening to the proceedings."

"From what realm?" asked Atkinson.

Dixie looked up at Atkinson and said, "The Dark Realm, Sire."

At this point, Dewhirst came in and said, "Nothing has come out of the Dark Realm for over 2000 years...what makes you think it was from that realm?"

"I could sense it, Milord. I couldn't see it because it merged into the wall."

"Did it know you had sensed it?"

"No, Sire. The pulses that it gave off didn't alter; I was monitoring it the whole time I was there."

"Report your findings to Tamara at once. You have done well," said Dewhirst.

"Thank you, Sire!"

"Remember, it is just thank you," said Atkinson.

"Sorry, Sire," said Dixie as she depressed the 'T' button on her phone, but stayed where she was.

"I'm already here, Dixie," said Tamara, as she walked in and knelt in front of Dewhirst. "Welcome back, Milord," she said.

"The 'Milord' thing, it's never going to change, is it?" said Atkinson.

Both Tamara and Dixie shook their heads.

"So be it," sighed Atkinson.

"Listmaker, take your apprentice and discuss your next move on the police officer; leave the Dark Realm to us," instructed Dewhirst.

Tamara and Dixie disappeared back to the Plane of Existence and reappeared in John Smith's office.

The two Gods of Death looked at each other. Atkinson, now deep in thought said, "I thought the battling would have stopped now that everything is in its place."

"No, my friend, the beings from the Dark Realm will try and take over while we are in this transitional state. Also, they know the Child of Nature has been born, so it is the optimum time for them to strike," said Dewhirst.

In the Reaper's office, the two Listmakers were sitting drinking tea when John Smith walked in.

"Hello, what are you two up to?"

"We have a police-person to disgrace," said Tamara.

"Poor chap, he doesn't know what's about to hit him," said Smith.

"What do you mean? We are good girls!" said Tamara.

"Exactly! Our Mr. Crawshaw deserves your special attention after what Paul told me about him. Now that you are both here, I have a question for you."

"Fire away," said Tamara.

"What do you know of shadowy demons? It turns out Gavin has had one going through his drawers," said Smith.

"How positively uncomfortable for him." said Tamara.

"You see, I knew as soon as those words left my lips you were going to say something like that..." said Smith.

Tamara just smiled, and Dixie said, "I have sensed it in Crawshaw's office, too."

"It is from the Dark Realm," informed Tamara.

"And what, pray tell, is the 'Dark Realm'?" enquired Smith.

"The short explanation is that when you reap the soul of a bad person – like a murderer, for instance, there is no rebirth into Humanity, so the soul is stripped and placed in safe keeping. The soul then placed in..."

"In the Dark Realm?" interrupted Smith.

"Yes," answered Tamara.

"So why is it here and not in its realm?" asked Smith.

"The Dark Realm wants the child. If said child is brought up in that realm, it will be just as powerful, but it will destroy rather than mend," said Tamara.

"Where does Chief Inspector Crawshaw fit into all of this?"

"That is what Dixie is working on. It will need a body to exist within this realm, so it will choose one that is not of good virtue – and he perfectly fits the bill," explained Tamara.

"So, what we are dealing with here is pure evil, but it doesn't have a form, so it will consume Chief Inspector Crawshaw?" said Smith.

"If it hasn't already – how could you tell the difference between Crawshaw and pure evil?" said Tamara.

"Compared to the creatures that exist in the Dark Realm, Crawshaw is an angel," said Dixie.

"Well, let's hope more of them don't follow, then," said Smith.

The two Listmakers just looked at each other, and then Tamara said, "Mark my words, this is just the beginning."

Back in his office, Chief Inspector Crawshaw was going over what had happened that afternoon. A strange lunch date from hell...but the promise of greatness! Oh yes, he would be the one who settled the cases that no one else could! Then something caught his eye, and the room darkened. A mist of swirling blackness came from the wall and engulfed him. A heavy feeling of dread and despair took over his being. It felt like he couldn't breathe, and he began to feel dizzy. It all became too much for him to bear, and he passed out on the floor. The evil had found its new host to be very welcoming, and merged with ease within its unconscious body.

Time passed in Crawshaw's office, and the air was heavy with crushing despair and hate. The man that was sitting in the chair had been totally engulfed by that long-dormant evil, and was ready to begin his work. But now he belonged to a new Master.

Chapter Seven

In the Realm of Nature, the first meeting was being held by the Centaurs as to the protection of the child. Both the change at the top level within the Realm of Death and the emergence of the being from the Dark Realm on the Plane of Existence had been duly noted. Both Mother Nature and the High Council of the Centaurs were pleased that Dewhirst was back where he belonged. His love of her creatures had been well-documented, and now he had partnered with a less aggressive Atkinson.

The fact remained, however, that the child was vulnerable during his first weeks of life, and if anything happened to him, Nature's full destructive power would be released upon the world with no compassion shown.

Mother Nature instructed the Centaurs to destroy anything that came close to the infant, and that they should guard him until their deaths. The power of the Centaurs was legendary, and their devotion to their Creator was unsurpassed. They would guard this child to their very extinction.

Mother Nature felt more at ease after the meeting, because there was something else to consider. She had put great strength into two Earth Children – the Guardian of the Earth and her spouse, the Sentinel. The birth of the couple's Saviour Child in the Realm of Nature had increased their personal power a hundredfold, and together they had become more powerful than any who had walked the Plane of Existence before them. *Should something happen to the child, what havoc would they wreak upon her world?*

In the Pathology Department at the hospital, Sarah (the most powerful being in existence) was doing a handstand against the wall, with her skirt tucked into her knickers, when Tom Harper walked into the room.

"God Almighty! What are you doing now, you strange beast?"

"I'm practicing yoga!" replied Sarah.

"This is a Mortuary; we are here to find out why the people in our fridges are here! We are not here to tuck our skirts into our pants and parade upside-down against the wall!"

"It's alright for you, you wear trousers so your underpants would not show if you did this," was Sarah's upside-down answer.

Gavin was on his mobile phone looking out of his office window, and saw Tom talking to Sarah's feet. Feeling he must investigate this strange happening, he came out into the main room. Taking the phone away from his ear, he said, "Is everything okay?"

Sarah smiled and nodded her head, banging it against the wall and collapsing in a heap on the ground. Tom just shook his head and said, "I wonder if she behaves like this at college?"

"I don't suppose so – I think she acts more like a student while she's there," said Gavin.

The two men stood looking at Sarah, who was now in a position that looked like she was halfway through a forward roll, only backwards.

"Oh God, you mean she's even worse there?" said Tom.

Gavin just nodded his head and went back to his office, continuing his phone call.

"Get up! You look ridiculous!" said Tom.

"The way I look is better than being an old grump!"

"There was no messing about when I was at university!" instructed Tom.

"That's why you're an old grump!" retorted Sarah.

"You're a juvenile!" said Tom.

"Grump!" said Sarah, as she got up and pulled her skirt out of her knickers.

"And put your white coat on, Gorezilla,"

"Grumpula!" said Sarah, blowing a raspberry.

Gavin looked out at his team. One of them held a PHD...and the other was a student that had just taken her skirt from inside her pants, both calling each other names...and the PHD was losing.

Gavin pondered for a moment upon the wonderful contradiction that was his wife. The girl that was pulling her skirt from her pants and blowing a raspberry was one and the same as the woman who had saved Humanity. He wondered what more was to come from this beautifully simple, fun-loving Goth girl who had stolen his heart.

In the Reaper's office, a discussion was taking place between the Reaper and two Listmakers.

"Normally, you would be left to deal with whatever crisis that emerged during your term as John Smith's Listmaker, but this is different to what you would normally expect," informed Tamara.

"In what way?" asked Dixie.

"It is no longer Chief Inspector Crawshaw that you are dealing with – this is now an entity from the Dark Realm, and it is here solely to find the whereabouts of the child."

"Can't we just kill it?" asked Smith.

"No – if we were to do that, the Elders of the Dark Realm would know we were onto them, and they would quickly release their Army of Despair to kill indiscriminately. Only then would we be able to use force, but as the battle raged, the loss to Humanity would be great," answered Tamara.

"How did it escape from that realm in the first place?" asked Dixie.

"That is a good question...I don't know the answer to it," said Tamara.

"So, we have to sit back and leave it free to roam?" asked Dixie.

"No, and here is where we have an advantage. We know that the creature will have now engulfed Chief Inspector Crawshaw. His thoughts will merge with its limited and controlled ones; this means the creature from the Dark Realm will carry on what Crawshaw has been doing. With this in mind, we can get it to spend more time with you, Dixie. I will take over the list-making, while you carry on your work with Chief Inspector Crawshaw. That way, we stay ahead of the game. While the beings from the Dark Realm have strength in numbers, singularly, they are weak and quite easy to manipulate. You should be able to find out its whereabouts quite easily and stay in control of the situation," said, Tamara.

"How do I stop it from discovering me?" asked Dixie.

"My darling, to human males, you are a devastatingly beautiful woman...and with my experience with the male of the species known as Humanity, they lose the ability to think when faced with such beauty as yours, my dear. In other words, use what the Gods gave you. He and whatever controls him will be putty in your hands."

"Do you mind, I'm male," said Smith.

"No you're not, you are an Immortal. We have no gender – we just use whatever gender we require dealing with our needs," corrected Tamara.

"In that case, why am I aroused whenever I'm with Tom Harper?" asked John Smith.

"Are you?" asked Dixie.

"Dixie, everyone knows about John and Tom Harper! You fancy him because he is cute and intelligent. Not bound by the stupid misgivings as to what is right or wrong, you enjoy what pleases you," informed Tamara.

"Why would it be wrong for me to fancy Tom?" asked Smith.

"We know it isn't wrong, but there are so many people in the world that would fight such a union, because to them it is 'unnatural'; and then, they would carry on with their surgically-enhanced women, and eat their genetically-modified foods," said Tamara.

The conversation went on about the rights and wrongs in the world, and eventually a plan hatched so that Dixie could start her work properly on the Chief Inspector…and his unusual guest.

In the Other Realm, Atkinson and Dewhirst were discussing the problem of the visitor from the Dark Realm.

"Have you battled this enemy before?" asked Atkinson.

"I have on occasions had to deal with the Dark Realm; your father and I are the ones who made that realm, and sometimes have had to defend this realm against it. Removing negativity is never an easy thing. When Humankind gained its awareness after the visitors mated with the primates, it did not show the tranquillity of the visitors. The first hybrids were angry and possessive. The visitors tried to educate early humanoids, but to no avail. After a time, they gave up on Homo Erectus, and left them to their fate by leaving the planet, presumably to go back to their world. The experiment, in their eyes, was a complete failure," he continued.

"Yes, my father told me about this," said Atkinson.

"The thing was, the visitors had taught them how to make tools for building, and weapons for hunting, but the new humans began to use the weapons on themselves. It wasn't too long before the species learned that violence meant power. For the first time, we were dealing with a species that would kill indiscriminately as an organized group, and these power-crazed humans began to lay waste to anything that stood in their way. For the first time as Reapers, we had to deal with negative energy at death. In an attempt to stop this energy from passing to the next life linked with the soul, we separated it at the reaping, and placed it into a separate realm – a realm that no one could penetrate, a realm that would hold all the negative energy until it dissipated," informed Dewhirst.

"We are going to have to come up with a plan, because thousands of years' worth of built-up hate is not a good thing to keep in one place. The destruction of the Dark Realm is long overdue," said Atkinson.

"I agree. Your father, however, wanted this to happen. He wanted all that built-up hate released upon the world."

"My father was a lunatic, his lust for power knew no bounds," answered Atkinson.

"For some strange reason, your father took pleasure in seeing the humans turn on themselves. Other dominant species long before and including the dinosaurs attacked each other, but it wasn't indiscriminate – it was for food or their place within society. The humans had turned this into a power struggle, and it wasn't long before the hunting parties had turned into armies, and as for the rest, you already know."

At the police station, Chief Inspector Crawshaw was feeling better than he had in years. He, for some reason, now had a purpose, and knew he must fulfil that purpose. *It must be Dixie,* he thought to himself. Dixie, however, was the vehicle the entity from the Dark Realm was going to be using to gain access to the Realm of Nature. The Chief Inspector looked at the business card Dixie had left, and he began to dial the number.

In the Other Realm, Atkinson saw Dixie's number being dialled and intercepted the call. Answering in Dixie's voice, he said, "Hello?"

"Hello, Dixie – I am sorry about my behaviour earlier; I would like to make things better between us. Would you come for a picnic with me?"

"Of course, I would," answered Atkinson.

"I will pick you up at your work," said the Chief Inspector.

"I will be ready in one hour," was the reply.

The calm afternoon at Atkinson, Dewhirst & Smith was interrupted by the arrival of Atkinson in the Reaper's office.

"You are making good use of this 'us being allowed on the same plane' thing," quipped Smith.

"Cute," replied Atkinson. "We have a breakthrough," he continued.

"Does it involve me, Milord?" asked Dixie.

"Very intuitive Dixie…yes, it does," answered Atkinson.

"I will do anything, Milord," offered Dixie.

"The Dark Realm has totally engulfed Crawshaw, and he wants to get into the Realm of Nature."

"I will do my best to keep him out of there," answered Dixie.

"That is what I want it to look like you are doing."

"I don't understand, make it 'look like' I am keeping him out?" Dixie replied.

"Yes, make it look like you are trying to keep him out. I want Crawshaw to believe he is tricking you, and that way we get the entity, Crawshaw and you all together once he is in there," informed Atkinson.

"I see," said Dixie.

"Wouldn't it be safer just to deal with it here and keep the Dark Realm away from the Realm of Nature and the child?" asked Smith.

"The Plane of Existence has had enough to deal with since the turn of the new millennium, and I am not sure it would survive another onslaught," said Atkinson.

"How dangerous can one entity be?" asked Smith.

"A battle with the Dark Realm on the Plane of Existence would be disastrous, so if there is a conflict, I want to fight them in their realm – not yours," advised Atkinson.

"I see, why do we have to sort this out? Why can't Mother Nature take care of this now that the child is in her care?" asked Smith.

"The Dark Realm has nothing to do with Nature, unfortunately. It was my father's idea of a good storage place for souls that needed their negativity removed. The trouble is, he just left them there, and never got around to coming up with a soul-cleansing idea. All the hatred and despair has just festered in this awful realm," advised Atkinson.

"And this is the realm you want to send Dixie into?" asked an incredulous Smith.

"Yes. The child, although powerful, will not be able to direct us. I need one of us in there as a beacon for us to attach to," answered Atkinson.

"It is fine – I am more than willing to do this. It will help Tamara to trust me totally, and I am not at all scared," said Dixie.

"Brave words, Dixie, I like that. But believe me, if we don't find you, you will be scared," answered Atkinson.

Dixie stood firm, and if she held any fear, she certainly wasn't showing any of it.

"And so it begins. The Chief Inspector will be picking you up here in 35 minutes. His intention is for you to take him into the Realm of Nature. Remember, you are not dealing with a simple human anymore. Do not make it obvious when you give in and take him there, we do not want the entity knowing we are onto them," said Atkinson.

"You can count on me, Sire," she said.

"I know I can," said Atkinson.

"So can I!" said Tamara, as she appeared in the office.

"What are you doing here?" asked Atkinson.

"In case we all forget, there are lists to make, and the Reaper must reap his souls, so while Dixie is doing what she's doing for you, I will be doing what she would be doing for the Reaper," said Tamara.

"If this is going to keep happening, I'm going to need a bigger office," said Smith.

"Can I have a word, darling?" said Tamara to Atkinson.

"Of course, you can! Now all this depends on you, Dixie," said Atkinson, as he depressed a button on his phone, and he and Tamara disappeared.

"You'd better get yourself ready, Dixie, it would appear you have another quest on your hands," said Smith.

Atkinson and Tamara re-emerged in the Other Realm.

"You have my absolute attention," said Atkinson.
"Permission to speak freely?" asked Tamara.
"Of course."
"What the hell do you think you're doing!" shouted Tamara.
"I granted permission to speak, not permission to scream."
"It should have been me going into that realm, not Dixie!"
"You are too valuable to lose," answered Atkinson.
"It's the Dark Realm we are talking about here, not a jaunt over the ocean of someone's mind! She is not ready for such a thing!"
"She was my choice, which means she is ready; we only need her to stay alive long enough for us to find the nucleus of the realm."
"Is she aware that she stays there if killed there?"
"And what would be the point in telling her that?" enquired Atkinson.
"So that she knows and understands the risks!" answered Tamara.
"She is going, Listmaker, and that is the end of this conversation."
"I'm not sure that only Dewhirst came back – you sound like your father! May I leave now, Sire?"
"I am not like my father...and stop calling me Sire! Yes, it is risky – but it's not only Dixie going into that realm, we all are, except for you and Dewhirst!"
"No! I refuse to be the one left behind!" demanded Tamara.
"As you so rightly pointed out to me, the list-making and reaping must carry on," advised Atkinson.
"Check the scrolls that told you that you were the Chosen One. The same scroll states that the Reaper and the Scribe stay in their realm in these cases. You may be my Lord, but you have to follow the rules, as we all do, Reaper."

"John Smith is a Reaper, too," said Atkinson.

"He may be, but you are The Reaper."

A short, uncomfortable silence followed, but was interrupted by the entrance of Dewhirst.

"Did I hear my name being shouted out?"

"I beg your pardon, Milord," said Tamara, bowing her head.

"I will not have this kind of subordination from a Listmaker in our Realm! However, Atkinson, she is right – not about sending the Listmaker into the Dark Realm though, she is the most inexperienced, so if you are going to lose anybody, it would be best if it was her. She is right about you and I not going there. We must trust our Warriors to do their duty while we keep things moving here. Furthermore, it would not be a good idea for the son of the one who put those wretched souls into that hell to go strolling through it, now, would it?" said the wise old Deity, albeit from a young-looking god.

"Sorry Tamara, and thank you for pointing that out," acquiesced Atkinson.

"You truly are not your father; he never made mistakes...or should I say, he never acknowledged them," said Dewhirst.

Tamara smiled, and said she was sorry, too.

Back on the Plane of Existence, Dixie bid goodbye to Smith and left his office. She tapped on her soon-to-be husband's door.

"Hello, darling!" greeted Johnson.

"We need to talk," answered Dixie.

"This sounds ominous," said Johnson.

"Yes, and no," was the strange reply.

"You have my undivided attention."

"I may be gone for a while; I have work to do in another realm. You are now one of us, so you have to understand that I must do this."

"I take it this is dangerous work, or we wouldn't be having this conversation," answered Johnson.

"It is, my love. But my strength will keep me safe, and your love will bring me back," reassured Dixie.

"Do I need to know what is involved?"

"No. You just need to know I must do this, and I am quite capable of doing it. This will be our life together, because there will be times when our roles reverse, and it will be me here, and you sorting things out on another plane," said Dixie.

"Well, my love, may the Gods watch your back, and return you to me soon. When do you have to leave?"

"I am leaving now...I will return," said Dixie.

Johnson rose from his chair, took his soul mate in his arms, and the pair kissed. He whispered in her ear, "I love you."

The part of Dixie's psyche that had become human began to let tears well up in her eyes, but the warrior within her held them back as she gave Johnson a smile and said, "I love you too darling, and I will be back."

John Smith was sitting at his desk with Tamara sitting opposite him. She looked radiant as she scribbled away on the list of that evening's nearly-departed. Sensing his attention, she looked up.

"Is there something amiss, John?"

"Nope, not at all...just..."

Tamara put her pen down and said, "What's on your mind?"

"Why has Dixie gone on this dangerous mission when you were far more qualified to do it?"

"I asked the same question of Atkinson. The answer is that it is his wish that Dixie performs this task," answered Tamara.

John Smith just looked down at his documents and fiddled with his pen. Still looking at him, Tamara said, "There is something else – come on John, what is on your mind?"

"It's something that has been preying on my mind, and it has begun to take up too much of my thinking."

"Oh, I see...you know perfectly well that Dixie can handle this; it's not about Dixie at all, is it John?"

"I am spending too much time thinking about Tom Harper," he confessed.

"The time you spend in the Realm of Death needs your entire attention. The time you spend out of there is your own, to think about whatever or whoever you want. But remember, you can have whoever you want, there are no rules," said Tamara.

"Is what I'm doing wrong? I know nothing of this kind of thing," said Smith.

"I've just said there are no rules. Humans are the worst when it comes to mating; they must follow rules that supposedly were laid down centuries ago by man. The act of lovemaking, as they like to put it, knows nothing of rules...it is an emotion. You follow your heart; it is that simple. Some of my most sensitive and passionate moments have been in the grip of a woman's embrace!" said Tamara.

"So what you are saying is, if it feels good, do it?"

"No, I'm saying, if it feels right, do it."

"Thank you. So, it doesn't matter if the Reaper is gay?"

"It would only matter if Hollywood ever found out about you; it would not match their idea of your appearance...you know...the skull, bony finger, black ragged-hooded cloak and scythe. They would have you wearing a rainbow-coloured cloak, and that would not be good for your image, darling," said Tamara.

The Reaper and Listmaker both burst into spontaneous laughter as Tamara picked up her pen and began writing again.

Chapter Eight

om Harper was in the examination room taking all the fluffy animal heads off his pens and pencils for the seventh time that week when Sarah walked in.

"Why are you taking those off of the pens? I like them!" protested Sarah.

"In that case, put them on the top of your pens, not mine."

"My pens are full – they've all got one on!"

"Sarah, this is a scientific examination room, where we find out why people have died. Some people might think a more sombre approach to our work is befitting."

"Why?"

"Because of respect for the dead."

"Why?"

"Because, we don't want doctors, police officers, or anyone else for that matter who has to call in here thinking that we are unprofessional."

"Why do my pencil tops make us unprofessional?"

"Because they do! Now go away you, little monster!"

"Why?

Tom gave Sarah that certain look he used when he was about to shout 'Gavin' so she made a quick retreat, giggling.

A little later, Gavin called Sarah into his office.

"Are you feeling okay, Sarah?"

"I think I'm feeling what you're feeling," she answered.

"Something is happening – I feel like I did just before I went to the portal," said Gavin.

"Yes, it came over me a few minutes ago, it has something to do with the Realm of Nature. I know that Tamara is back at the office, for some reason," said Sarah.

"I think we had better find out," answered Gavin.

Both depressed the 'Tamara' button on their phones, and transported themselves to John Smith's office.

"I've been expecting you two," said Tamara.

"What has happened?" asked Sarah.

"Dixie is about to take your office intruder into the Realm of Nature, and then follow it into the Dark Realm."

"Isn't that dangerous for the child, taking it in there?" asked Gavin.

"Yes, but he has good protection while he's in there; it is when they are all transported into the Dark Realm that he will be most at risk," answered Tamara.

Both Sarah and Gavin looked shocked and puzzled at Tamara's last statement.

"The Dark Realm has become over-populated and unstable; its very existence was never a good idea. If we don't deal with it now, there may be no reason to have the child, because if that Realm spills over into this Realm, there will be no hope for Humankind as it will feed on greed, want and lust. It will combine with the worst kind of humans and then totally devour them, turning father against son, mother against daughter. In fact, the whole human race would be at war with itself, and it would be a war to extinction," stated Tamara.

The look of shock and puzzlement had changed to one of horror as Sarah said, "What do you want us to do?"

"As soon as Dixie gets into the Dark Realm, we will all meet up and follow her inside. Once there…"

"Once there you draw your swords and kill everything you see!" interrupted Atkinson as he appeared in the office.

"A simple enough plan," said Smith.

"You go into the Dark Realm and fix your attentions on the strongest source of power – that will be either the child or the main gathering of Dark Souls. You make your way to that power source, and the more you kill on the way, the stronger the signal will be that the child gives off. Be ready, the call can come at any minute, depending upon how long it takes Dixie to get there," instructed Atkinson.

"Will Dixie be with the child?" asked Sarah.

"I don't know," answered Atkinson. "She may be put to the sword as soon as she arrives in the Dark Realm, as she may be surplus to requirements," he continued.

"But you will be able to bring her back, won't you?" asked Sarah.

"No. Anyone dispatched in that realm stays in that realm," said Atkinson.

"And you're okay with that?" asked Smith.

"We are all expendable," instructed Atkinson.

After being picked up by Crawshaw, Dixie sat in the passenger seat feeling quite relaxed. She knew what lay ahead, and had accepted the conditions of the job in hand. She knew that if she worried about it, the Entity controlling Crawshaw would soon discover her intentions...and she certainly didn't want that. Looking at the driver, she said, "Where are we going for lunch?"

"The pub just down the road from the police station," said Crawshaw, in a direr tone than usual.

Dixie looked at him closely; it was as if the unknown entity that had engulfed him was showing its true self, because he really was the worst human she had ever encountered.

"Sounds wonderful! What are we doing afterwards, going back to your place?"

"No!" was his quick response.

Dixie was rather pleased with his answer, because she wasn't looking forward to any carnal acts with him before the possession with this thing, and he seemed even worse now.

"In that case, what are we doing?

"Let's just eat and see what happens," replied Crawshaw.

They drove on to the public house, and once inside, perused the menu. Looking up from the list of simple pub food, Dixie noticed the Chief Inspector was sweating quite profusely.

"Are you alright, my dear?" asked Dixie.

"I'm fine. What do you want to eat?" was the gruff reply.

"Well, I'm torn between the meat pie and chips, the pasty and chips, or the fish and chips," said Dixie, wondering if they did chips and chips as their special.

"Make your mind up, we haven't got all day," said Crawshaw.

"In that case, I will have the fish...without the chips, if that's okay."

"Please yourself," said Crawshaw, as he made his way to the bar to order the food.

As well as the fact that Crawshaw was sweating, he was emitting a rather nasty odour, the likes of which she had never experienced before. His skin was turning ever-so-slightly darker, and dark rings were appearing around his eyes. As a couple, they looked odd...because she was devastatingly beautiful, and he was growing uglier by the minute. He came back with two pints of lager, and roughly placed one in front of her, spilling some of its contents.

Dixie looked up at him and said, "If you want this date to go any further, you are going to have to change your attitude and the way you look...I think I deserve a bit more respect than I am receiving."

With that, as if startled, Crawshaw got up and calmly walked to the Gent's toilet. Once inside, the entity exited him and took residence within the circuitry of his mobile phone.

The dark shadows cleared from his eyes and the smell dispersed. He was a bit disoriented, suddenly finding himself in the Gent's toilet, but had a vague idea of what was happening. He rinsed his face in the hand sink and dried himself off. The sweating had stopped, and the moist dark patches that had appeared under the arms of his jacket disappeared. He, in fact, looked quite good in the reflection of the mirror In front of him. Straightening his tie, he smirked back at himself and rejoined his date.

Dixie noticed he was back as Crawshaw, but knew the entity was nearby. Not letting her inner thoughts give away any information about her knowledge of the beast, she smiled, and said, "You look much better darling. Were you feeling unwell?"

"I did come over a bit faint, but I feel fine now," he replied. "Now, where were we?" asked Dixie.

"Shall we go for a walk in the woods after lunch?" suggested the Chief Inspector.

"Well, that depends on whether I will be safe or not, doesn't it, Chief Inspector?"

"Of course, you'll be safe," he replied.

"I don't know if I want to be safe," she teased.

"Oh...I see; we can see what develops when we are in the woods."

"In that case, I would love to go for a stroll in the woods with you!" said Dixie.

Crawshaw ate his lunch and Dixie had a few morsels of fish. Little over ten minutes had passed when Crawshaw said "Shall we go, then?"

The couple stood up and left the rather dismal public house and got back into the car. The experience of the food had done nothing to stay in Dixie's memory, although the Chief Inspector had devoured his pie and chips.

The drive to the woods was quite pleasant by the standards she had come to expact from her time spent with the Chief Inspector.

As the car pulled up in a lay-by at the edge of the wooded area, Crawshaw said, "If we are going to have any romance, we need to get the questions out of the way, first."

"Questions, Chief Inspector?"

"My questions concerning your dealings with Atkinson, Dewhirst & Smith...and a certain matter of me closing the case on them."

"The case is not against the new company, it is against Atkinson, Atkinson and Dewhirst," informed Dixie.

"That makes no difference to me," said Crawshaw.

"What would you like to know?"

"You have told me you have documented evidence placing Atkinson at the scenes of all the unsolved murders."

"Yes, I do," said Dixie.

"You are not just a secretary, are you?" probed Crawshaw.

"I think we both know the answer to that question," answered Dixie.

"You could be setting me up," quipped Crawshaw.

"Setting you up for what, Chief Inspector?"

"This whole thing could be an elaborate plot to get your boyfriend back in his old job."

"Oh, please – you are safe in your job. My boyfriend, as you call him, is quite happy doing what he's doing," replied Dixie.

"Okay, I will set a little test first, to see if you are who I think you are, and if you can demonstrate what you can do."

"Really, Chief Inspector? This is starting to get boring,"

"Shall I address you as Dixie, or should I call you Listmaker?"

"You can call me Joan of Arc, if it pleases you!" said Dixie.

"Come now, Listmaker, clearly I know who you are, and I also know how you people can move between different realms."

"If you know all this, why do you need me? It sounds like you already have enough to go marching in with the 'boys in blue' and close the place down!"

"Indeed, I do...and believe me, I will close that dismal place down! But first, you can give me the one thing that will seal the deal."

"And what is that, Chief Inspector? I'm afraid you're a little late if it's my virginity you require,"

"Hardly, I need evidence of one of the different realms."

"Are you out of your mind?" laughed Dixie.

At that point, the entity slipped back into Crawshaw, and his face altered.

"I am not out of my mind, and you will take me into another realm!"

Dixie knew the entity was back in charge, but kept her vital signs perfectly normal as she said, "In that case, why don't I take you to the Other Realm...and we can take tea with Atkinson."

The dark entity inside Crawshaw made him recoil with fear.

"No! Not...not that realm!" he stuttered.

"Would you like to take your chances in the Realm of Death, Chief Inspector?" Dixie asked with a grin.

"No! Not that one, either! I just want to go to a nice realm that is different to this one."

Knowing she couldn't mention the Dark Realm, she said the only realm that she could use.

"The only realm left is the Realm of Nature."

Crawshaw, who was now looking dark-eyed again, said, "Yes! Take me there!"

"But what good will taking you to another realm do? What will it prove? And what happens if Atkinson finds out that I have taken you there?" said Dixie, making him work all the way.

"It will be our secret," said Crawshaw.

"Tomorrow...I will take you there tomorrow," said Dixie.

"Now! I need to go there now!" insisted Crawshaw as he began sweating again.

"You will have to be patient, Chief Inspector...one more day won't hurt, now will it?" teased Dixie.

Again, in the shadows, Atkinson stood monitoring the situation, a situation that Dixie seemed to have perfectly under control.

The drive back was sullen, and Dixie could feel the hate emanating from Chief Inspector Crawshaw. Even his expression was changing. He was looking older, and his scowl had become more intense. His odour was becoming unbearable, and she opened the car window for some fresh air. The whole atmosphere in the car was now heavy, and she wished the drive back would soon be over. As the car came to an abrupt halt at the offices of Atkinson, Dewhirst & Smith she quickly alighted.

"Tomorrow, at 9:30 a.m., sharp!" said the gruff-voiced Chief Inspector.

"12:30 p.m.," said Dixie, as she turned and walked towards the building.

The Chief Inspector's car sped off, and Dixie made her way to the main door. Once inside, Dixie acknowledged the Sunny Acres mob and went straight to John Smith's office. Upon entering, she was greeted by both Smith and Atkinson.

"Well done, Dixie," said Atkinson. Smith just smiled.

"Thank you, my Lord," answered Dixie, bowing her head.

"You are doing the 'my Lord' thing again, but I must say, you are doing well my dear – I liked the way you handled the situation," announced Atkinson.

"I am glad you approve, Sire; I did feel your presence," said Dixie.

"Let's just say, I was taking part in a quality control exercise, and you passed the test. Tomorrow is when the real work begins, and this path you will have to tread carefully, and alone," informed Atkinson.

"I am ready my Lord, and I will not let you down."

"I know this to be true, Dixie."

Atkinson returned to his realm, leaving only Smith and Dixie in the office.

"Tell me, Dixie, how do you feel about all of this?"

"Honoured, Sir," she replied.

"This could be a one-way ticket, Atkinson has no remorse about that," said Smith.

"I know, but not long ago, I was one of thousands of beings with little importance. Now, I can make a difference," replied Dixie.

"You already have," said Smith.

"I shall do this of my own free will. Tomorrow I will enter the Realm of Nature, then on to the Dark Realm...and I will return!" she stated.

Within the Realm of Nature, the child had begun to grow. He was a baby in human years, but he was now the size of a twelve-year-old boy. He was strong and intelligent. His time with the Centaurs had been well-spent. Much had he learned from these great beasts of the forest; his strength was as great as theirs. His understanding of things was very advanced, and the way he perceived situations matched the leader of the Centaurs...so much so that they could offer him no more, and what was supposed to take more than six full months had indeed taken less than six weeks.

The sky over the ring of purple-tipped mountains that stood as bastions to the Centaurs grew lighter as day broke magnificently. Great outstretched fingers of light dispersed the night sky, chasing away the bright stars. Birds began to sing their dawn chorus. The animals of the forest began to forage, and the leader of the Centaurs stood on a rock; on his back sat the child.

Both Centaur and child looked at an opening that was occurring in the trees in front of them, as the great oaks moved to create a pathway to their fortress stronghold. Fairy folk fluttered along the path, as if to check its safety. Wolves then followed, and lined the path on either side, as Mother Nature walked effortlessly into their kingdom.

All the creatures of the forest, including the Centaurs, kneeled before her and offered her praise. The child sitting on the Centaur's back looked on. His eyes were transfixed upon Mother Nature as she spoke.

"Creatures of the Ring of Mountains, hear me now!"
Every pair of eyes were glued to her and all ears pricked as the Goddess spoke.

"Nature's child has reached his first stage of development long before we expected. It is now time for his next step," she said as she walked over to the seated child, flowers growing from the places in the Earth where her feet had touched. As she moved to his position, birds flew around the three of them. She held out her hand to the boy. He took her hand, and slid himself off the leader of the Centaurs, who trotted away to join the gathered crowd. Mother Nature took the child in her arms, and embraced him.

A transference began to happen between the two, as a whirlwind twisted around them.

From the opposite end of the clearing, mighty oaks began to part again, as a very tall female warrior of immense power approached. Her attire was stunning. Knee-length, armour-plated boots were laced up the fronts of her long legs, which were clad in chain mail up to her tiny gladiator kilt. Her sword was missing from its scabbard, and its belt hung loosely down her left side. The chain mail continued over her body and down her arms. A golden breastplate, inscribed with lettering that told of her powers, and shoulder plates of shimmering gold with large spikes protruding from them, glinted in the sunlight. Upon her right hand was a golden gauntlet. Her crowning glory was her beautiful locks of blonde hair, long and flowing, dancing in the sunlight. finishing her attire was a hairband that looked more like a small crown.

Again, the animals knelt down as she walked into the vortex. As Sarah joined Mother Nature, they held hands around the child; both Mother Nature and Earth Mother began to chant the inscribed words from Sarah's breastplate, and their ancient knowledge was now shared with the growing child. The chanting continued from within the vortex as the child grew into a man...and what a man he was!

The vortex cleared, and three beings stood tall and proud. To his right stood Sarah, and to his left stood Mother Nature. The naked figure of Man that only Gods could produce surveyed his new domain.

He was taller than his two mothers, standing nine feet in height, a perfect specimen of raw manhood. His head was magnificent, with strong features, including a broad jawline. His eyes were ice blue with cat-like pupils. His eyelids looked as if they had eyeshadow on them, but, in fact, were the natural colour of the purple-topped mountains. His eyebrows were fair and curved the shape of his well-formed brow line. He had a perfectly-shaped nose – not too big and not too small – it resembled the nose of the Greek God Zeus. In fact, most of his features could be likened to that Grecian God of the Sky. Unlike Zeus, he was clean-shaven. His mouth was soft, with lips that were quite full for a man's. His hair was a shorter version of his Earth Mother's warrior-guise hair. It was golden and shoulder-length, and kept in place by a half-inch wide leather band tied at the back. He had very broad shoulders, heavy-set with muscle, and his gigantic back was a perfect V-shape as he narrowed at the waist. His chest was beautiful and matched his strong back; his pectoral muscles well-defined and taut, but not overly round. Just as his back, his chest was V-shaped down to his waist, but was chiselled over his emphasized abdominal musculature. He was narrow at the hips, and his buttocks were rock-hard. His phallus, although at rest, was a magnificent sight to behold, its length and girth in perfect scale to the rest of his huge body. He began to widen out again at his strong thighs, then narrowed at his calves. Apart from his large size, he looked like a human, albeit a perfect human, in every detail. He only differed in two ways – his hands and feet were webbed, and his eyes were cat-like.

From above, several golden eagles began to drop feathers upon him; snakes slithered to where he stood, and wrapped themselves around his legs, shedding their skins upon them. porcupines laid spines at his feet, and the fairies covered him in webbing spun by the industrious arachnids of the forest. Mother Nature raised her hand, and all the different materials began to fuse together all over his body, making a suit of clothing like no other ever crafted. The first lining of this incredible costume was a snakeskin bodysuit, enabling him to slide away into the smallest of hideouts. Covering that was chain mail made from super-strengthened porcupine needles. A covering of spider webbing ensuring strength and invisibility was next, should he need it. Upon each shoulder, a scattering of golden eagle feathers had been crafted, offering him flight. His two mothers looked upon him. and delighted in the image in front of them.

At the East side of the clearing, once again, the great oaks moved apart, and the sound of marching feet heralded another entrance. An army of soldier ants filed into the clearing. With them walked Gavin, carrying a helmet made of gold, in the same design of his Earth Mother's crowning headpiece. A spear just like the staff of Mother Nature's came next, and then the third and final piece was a shield like the one Tamara used.

The weapons, when used together, would now wield the strength of four of the most powerful beings in existence.

He graciously accepted the weapons, placing the helmet upon his head, the shield upon his arm, and the spear in his hand.

All of the animals who had gathered to witness this unprecedented event began to look to the West side of the clearing, as for the fourth and final time the great oaks began to part. The sound of hooves could be heard, clip-clopping down the new pathway and into the clearing. Following Tamara was Juliantrium, a beautiful grey-winged unicorn with a flowing white mane and tail, who trotted behind Tamara like the world's greatest dressage pony.

The unicorn, who towered above Tamara, stared at the being in the middle of the opening as Tamara knelt in front of him, saying, "To the man who people will follow, the one who will save the planet, I offer you Juliantrium. She will be your travel partner, providing every transport you will ever need. She is a Shape-Shifter – she can morph into anything that is needed to assist you from now on." Tamara handed the reins to him and withdrew.

Mother Nature looked at Juliantrium and gave her a loving smile. She then turned back to the Earth Mother, and with her stepped forward, and shouted, "Humankind has now received its last chance to survive!" Both she and Sarah lifted their offspring's hands aloft, and said in unison, "We present to you, Paladin!"

The animals of the forest moved closer to him, touching him gently with their wet noses. Each one of them wanted to be near him. His two mothers let go of his hands, and the animals took him into the clearing and gathered around him. He smiled and spoke softly in a language they all seemed to understand. Mother Nature and Earth Mother looked on, then turned to each other and embraced.

"He has a duty to perform, and will join you in your realm," said Mother Nature.

"My realm needs him for sure," answered Sarah.

"Indeed it does, but he must tread a darker path first," informed Mother Nature.

"Why?"

"He must help right a very old wrong. Once done, his work on the Plane of Existence will begin."

JOHN PAUL BERNETT

Chapter Nine

ay broke in the most beautiful fashion as Dixie gazed at her sleeping soul mate. She edged closer to him and kissed his lips. He awoke and saw her through his dazed, sleepy eyes. He smiled and said, "Good morning." She just kissed him again, as he put his arms around her naked shoulders. The window was open, and the chirping of songbirds and smells of fragrant flowers filled the room.

Paul embraced Dixie and pulled her on top of himself, allowing his hands to wander down to her peach-like bottom, which he very gently squeezed. Her hair dangled onto his face as she smiled sweetly at him and kissed him again. His arousal was very noticeable to her, as she could feel the swelling of his love. The magnificence of the daybreak was matched by the power of his emotions as he kissed her neck and ear. Her arousal was such that it made her forget what she was going to be doing later that day – but that would be a different Dixie.

This Dixie could only think of her man; this man she could crush with one hand if she so desired, but would harm herself before she hurt a single hair on his head. She gently lifted herself up, so her breasts were in front of his face. He lavished all kinds of love and adoration upon their pert beauty. Her nipples showed their pleasure at his industrious, warm lips. She threw her head back and bit gently on her bottom lip as the pleasure intensified.

His kiss was deep, and full of love and devotion. She lifted her hips slightly, allowing his excited manhood to slip into her welcoming portal of pleasure. Very gently, he moved his hips forward, sliding his phallus deeply into her accepting vagina. She let her hands relax, and once again was face to face with her love, kissing him with the full extent of her passion. She rode him softly, swivelling her hips ever-so-gently. She looked into his now fully open eyes, and into his soul, and saw a reflection of pure love... love for just one person... her.

As they made love to the sounds of gentle moans and the songs of birds, Paul Johnson wanted this day to last forever. As she accepted his love graciously, she wished this day was over, and she was back on the Plane of Existence with her man, making love.

John Smith returned from the Realm of Death, and the great door creaked as it closed behind him.

"Good day at the office, dear?" asked Tamara as she passed him a cup of tea.

John Smith smiled and accepted the beverage.

"You look troubled," observed Tamara.

"A little," admitted Smith as he sat down at his desk.

"Trouble shared, and all that?" offered Tamara.

"Dixie..." said Smith, "I have been thinking about her all night," he continued.

"Dixie is merely doing her job, a job she is quite adequate to perform. Once she has Crawshaw in the Realm of Nature, her power will increase tenfold," said Tamara.

"Yes indeed – and won't that be the point where whatever is guiding Crawshaw will realise she isn't human?" asked Smith.

"Now that will depend upon Dixie. She has so far proven she can hide her emotions from the entity. You must remember, this entity has no real concept of right and wrong. It is just fulfilling a request from the Dark Realm. It will not detect her as an Immortal until it gets her back to its realm...at which time we will have a fix on her position."

"I don't like the sound of that Realm, or its inhabitants," said Smith.

"Don't worry about it, our Warriors will be up to the challenge," comforted Tamara.

Dixie and Johnson arrived at the firm, and both went to their respective offices as per the norm. For some reason, Johnson's 'in' tray was full, and would keep him busy for some time. Dixie, however, had a date with destiny as she walked into Smith's office.

"Good morning, Dixie, I hope you are well-rested," greeted Tamara.

"I am, thank you," she answered, bowing her head.

"Are you ready, my dear?" asked Smith.

"I am," she said with a smile.

"Are you fully up to speed on what you need to do?" asked Tamara.

As if at a loss for a different answer, Dixie replied again, "I am."

"And the risks – Dixie, do you fully understand the dangers?" asked Smith.

"My understanding of the dangers is neither here nor there; this is a job given to me by Atkinson. It will be done exactly to his specifications, whether I am afraid, or not. I am not human, so cannot be driven by emotions in matters such as this," explained Dixie.

The morning passed in its usual manner, and at exactly 12:30 p.m., the tooting of a car horn blasted from outside.

"He doesn't even have the decency to get out of his vehicle and call for you?" observed Smith.

"That is one of the many reasons the entity picked that vile worm of a man!" scoffed Tamara.

"I will be off then, wish me luck!" said Dixie.

"The very best of luck, my dear," said Smith.

"You won't need luck Dixie, you will be just fine," said Tamara, gently kissing her on the cheek.

Dixie almost forgot about the job at hand when that kiss touched her cheek. Up until a short time ago, she only knew the mythology about the Listmaker. She grew up like every other female, in awe of her power and standing within her company, and now she had received a kiss from her. With the largest smile on her face, she bid them goodbye as she left the office, and then the building, meeting her date in Crawshaw's waiting car.

The atmosphere in the car was thick, with the aroma of body odour and the feeling of deep depression. Crawshaw appeared unshaven, and looked like he hadn't slept.

"You hardly look ready for a nice walk in the forest," said Dixie, opening the window to let some fresh air into the car.

"We have work to do," was the simple answer.

The car sped off in the direction of the woods. Dixie kept her face close to the open window. Crawshaw by this point was certainly not in control of himself.

Paladin and his unicorn Juliantrium had bid goodbye to his mothers and the Centaurs, and made their way into the forest. Not really knowing his destination, he asked Juliantrium if she knew the way ahead.

"We are heading for your first of many pre-ordained meetings. This first meeting could prove to be most troublesome," said the magical unicorn.

"Ah...the Dark Realm..." said Paladin.

"You will be confronted with Good and Evil...and must tread warily, Paladin."

"Indeed, I shall...and if I need you to change, great unicorn?"

"You will see me change under you. I decide when the time is right for a change, that way, you can concentrate on what you need to do," informed Juliantrium.

"That makes perfect sense," said Paladin.

The two of them trotted on to the pre-destined meeting place within the Realm of Nature.

Dixie and Crawshaw, along with the entity controlling him, arrived at the edge of the woods. They chose a not-so-well-worn path. The area bore a canopy of trees that precious little light could penetrate. Passing ancient trees illuminated only by dappled sunlight, they came across a small opening amongst a copse of ferns.   An area of short grass with remnants of old standing stones circling the perimeter now stood in front of them. Dixie was the first to enter, followed by Crawshaw, who was catching the attention of all manner of flies and other assorted insects.

"What happens now?" enquired Crawshaw.

"Now, I ask you if this is what you really want to do...the Realm of Nature can be unfriendly...to certain individuals," noted Dixie.

"Yeah, yeah...get on with it!" was his morose answer.

Dixie stood in the middle of the clearing and telepathically called Tamara.   Tamara, in turn, asked permission both from Mother Nature and Atkinson to open the portal into the Realm of Nature. They both gave their permission, and a light appeared just before Dixie. The twinkling star-like shape began to spin, and very soon, an aperture into the Realm of Nature began to open.

As it opened further, its shape was that of a cat's eye – pointed at the top and bottom, but becoming quite wide at its centre. The darkness of the Plane of Existence was being chased away by the light emanating from the portal. The edge of the now fully-open entrance was shimmering like a beacon as Dixie stepped into the Realm of Nature. Looking back, she held her hand out to Crawshaw, who ignored it and just barged past her.

As soon as they stepped into that Realm, Crawshaw began to gasp for breath, as Nature's Realm quickly started to overpower him. He was dying, and if he did, the entity would die with him, and all the plans to stealthily infiltrate the Dark Realm would go too. Instinctively, Dixie took hold of Crawshaw and threw him back outside into the Realm of Existence, knowing the entity would engulf her. She was right. A dark, heavy, foreboding feeling of dread swallowed her whole being as its power grew in the Realm of Nature.

The entity realised it could use Dixie to survive until its return to the Dark Realm. The portal closed and the entity was where it wanted to be, and Crawshaw was now out of the equation on the Plane of Existence. He came to, and found himself deep in the woods alone, not knowing why he was there. Dazed, he began walking back up the dark path with just delicate fingers of light slightly illuminating it. After some time, he found himself back outside the woods by his parked car. Upon opening the door, he was greeted with the stench of body odour. He got inside and caught his image in the mirror, and wondered how he had gotten into such a state. He started the engine and drove away in the direction of his home, still not knowing what was happening, but very sure it had something to do with a particular accountancy firm...and he had had enough.

In the Other Realm, Atkinson realised something was wrong. He quickly ran to Dewhirst, who was sitting at his desk, scribbling names at an incredible rate. Dewhirst glanced up at Atkinson and said, "I felt it too, something has not gone to plan."

"Indeed...I was tracking Dixie all the way into the Realm of Nature, then I suddenly I lost her," stated Atkinson.

"There was always the possibility that this would happen...that is why we sent Dixie instead of Tamara."

"Yes, I am aware of that, but I don't share my father's ease of conscience with these matters," answered Atkinson.

"A few more millennia in the job will help you with that," remarked Dewhirst, "For now, we must find a different way of tracking the entity," he continued.

Atkinson was quite perplexed by this development, and was not quite sure what his next move would be. He looked at Dewhirst and said, "I'm going to call on an old friend...I won't be long."

With that, he disappeared, and Dewhirst returned to his writing.

"Welcome to my Realm, Atkinson," said Mother Nature, slightly bowing her head.

"Thank you for accepting me," replied Atkinson, offering the same bow.

"I give life – you take life; our paths don't usually cross," observed Nature.

"This is true, Milady, but this isn't official business."

"I wasn't aware the Reaper knew anything but 'official business'."

"I am not my father, and I do not approve of his way of working."

"You share his ruthless streak, the way you dispatched him."

"Milady, I did what needed doing – and nothing more."

"And now you are here," said Mother Nature, "wondering what has become of the warrior you sent into my Realm without permission!" she continued.

"Tamara sought your permission, Milady," offered Atkinson.

"Yes she did – the girl known as Dixie had my permission to enter...you failed to inform me that she was a Warrior."

"A misjudgement on my account, one that I hope can be forgiven. You are about to send a being from your Realm onto the Plane of Existence via the Dark Realm... both of which are my domains; I don't recall discussing this matter with you," answered Atkinson.

"Time is wasting, Reaper. State your business. I have many reasons not to trust you. My Realm – and my planet – have suffered much at the hands of the Atkinsons."

"As I have already said, I am different to my father."

"We shall see," answered Mother Nature.

"As you know, the Dark Realm was a folly of my father's making. It has now grown out of control. One of its inhabitants has recently been on the Plane of Existence, and now dwells in your Realm," stated Atkinson.

"I am aware of this."

"And you didn't eradicate it?"

"I saw who was with it, and knew it wasn't threatening my realm."

"Then you know my business, Milady. We intend to follow it into its realm, and put that entire realm to the sword," said Atkinson.

"What will you put in its place?"

"Our Well of Souls has enough to start again when the next dominant species evolves, so as of now, souls will have their essence of hate removed, and not stored for some future project of my father's. It will be dealt with as written, and so done, by the book," said Atkinson.

Mother Nature looked at him with a hint of approval in her eyes. "You have Dewhirst back with you...what if you bring back my husband? What then, Reaper?"

"I don't understand, Milady...your husband?"

"Yes...my husband. Did you never wonder who your mother was?"

Atkinson was silent for a moment, and then said, "My father was your husband?!"

"Work it out for yourself. Life and Death evolved as soon as the planet was ready to accept it. All you know began with your father and I; I have made everything, and your father – and now you, take it away – the first thing our union made was you."

Atkinson was stunned, but somehow, deep within his psyche, he knew what she had said to be true. He began to step backward as if to leave, when Mother Nature said, "The being known to you as Dixie has been engulfed by the entity you seek. As you already know, Paladin has matured."

She walked up to the son she had not seen in millions of years, and touched his face. She passed through her fingers the essence of Paladin. "Use that as your guide when he goes into the Dark Realm. Heed my word, Atkinson – make no move until they withdraw from my Realm. This audience is now over."

Atkinson was now in his realm, in a state of confusion.

"Why is what you have just learned causing you such problems, my old friend?"

"How can you say that? I have just found out that Mother Nature is my mother!"

"Technically, she is everyone's mother," said Dewhirst.

"I mean, literally!" said Atkinson.

"Apart from the part that said you were the 'Chosen One', have you ever read the Great Book of Existence?" inquired Dewhirst.

"No, I haven't," answered Atkinson.

Dewhirst just shook his head and said, "Never mind; we have our beacon now, and the entity is about to meet him."

In the Realm of Nature, Paladin sat astride Juliantrium as Dixie, or rather the being she had become, moved slowly towards him.

"Hello, traveller, what brings you along this path?" asked Paladin.

"I journey to meet you," said Dixie, her eyes closed and her lips motionless.

"I have been expecting you...come, rest awhile," he answered.

"My time here is limited, and I must return home," was the plea.

"I sense you are not of this realm; a lost soul, if you will?" comforted the being sat astride the unicorn.

Dixie lifted her head slightly and opened her eyes, outstretching her arm briefly, trying to connect with Paladin. As soon as their hands touched, the entity engulfed both rider and unicorn, causing Dixie to fall lifeless to the ground. A portal to the Dark Realm began to open at their side.

The unicorn leaped through the open ring within the fabric of the Realm's wall, and Paladin and Juliantrium were where the Master of the Dark Realm wanted them – within his domain, and under his power.

Mother Nature walked over to Dixie from her vantage point, and lifted the lifeless Warrior up in her arms. She cradled Dixie's head to her shoulder, and uttered an enchantment into the dead Warrior's ear. The forest grew quiet, as Mother Nature's tender embrace seemed to be taking the pained expression away from Dixie's face. A twitch of the girl's left eye was the first sign of rejuvenated life within her. Mother Nature kissed her forehead, and Dixie's eyes, as if waking from a slumber, opened.

"Welcome back, Dixie...be still. You are amongst friends."

As Nature said those words, the forest itself began to breathe again, as the sounds of Nature's Realm returned. A deer was the first animal to walk over and nudge Mother Nature. She sat Dixie back on the ground, and the little animal touched Dixie's face with its wet nose. Before she knew it, she was surrounded by a multitude of animals, all of whom wanted to touch the rejuvenated Warrior. Mother Nature held her hand out to Dixie, and as she took hold, the animals backed away, and Dixie transformed into Warrior mode.

"This will be the only time I will let one of Atkinson's Warriors into my Realm, as your fight is a just one," said Mother Nature, lifting her mighty staff and twirling it in a counter-clockwise ring in front of Dixie. "Dixie, you touched Paladin's hand – that touch will be like a beacon for you to follow. Now, join up with your friends, and deliver Paladin into your Realm."

The gateway to the Dark Realm began to open as Dixie readied herself. As soon as the aperture was large enough, she thanked Mother Nature with a smile and a nod of her head. She then jumped through without a second's thought for her safety.

In his office, Paul Johnson, who had just had the worst feeling of dread take over his entire being, was suddenly thrust into the most incredible feeling of adulation for his lover.

John Smith felt a surge through his body. He looked up at Tamara, whose eyes were wide open, showing obvious signs that she had just felt the same joyful experience.

Sarah ran into Gavin Jackson's office, bursting through the door. Gavin was already standing up, having had the same surge pass through him.

Atkinson and Dewhirst both looked at each other as Dewhirst dropped his quill. They both said together, "Dixie!"

Both Sarah's and Gavin's phones began to ring as the word 'Dixie' flashed on their respective displays. Instantly changing into Warrior mode, they depressed Dixie's button on their phones. They both materialised in the Dark Realm, standing on either side of the Warrior-clad Dixie.

"So...Mother Nature has allowed safe passage through her realm of one of our Warriors to help us?" said Dewhirst.

"Yes indeed; we must find a way to repay her," said Atkinson.

"As long as you don't pay me like your father did," a voice from behind them said.

They both spun around, and to their collective amazement, Mother Nature was standing in their domain.

"Mother Nature! You honour us with your presence!" said Dewhirst, slightly bowing his head.

"Mother!" said Atkinson.

"Dewhirst, you look well. It has been a long while since we last spoke."

"Too long!" replied the Scribe, "Your assistance in this matter is overwhelming!" he continued.

"It was ordained that we should work together. It wasn't I who put an end to that relationship..." said Nature.

"How can this be? You, being here in this realm with us?" said Atkinson.

"The same way you came into my Realm," replied Nature. "When you changed the rules, it wasn't just for the three realms that you work in, you changed the rules for us all. However, that enabled the dreadful soul from the Dark Realm to enter the Plane of Existence, and then with Dixie to get into my Realm," instructed Mother Nature.

"My reason for the change was made with good intentions, so that no other Deity could do what my father did," said Atkinson.

"You are showing concern for my creatures, and my world...perhaps there is more of me to your being than I realised. And you, Dewhirst – you thwarted my husband's plan to finish the human race, which means there is good in you. For this very reason, I decree a truce, and I grant safe passage through my Realm; safe passage, that is, as yourselves, not as Warriors. The Earth-Child Paladin is now in the Dark Realm – I am trusting you to bring him out unscathed."

"Dixie, now joined by the Sentinel and Paladin's Earth-Mother, will deliver Paladin and put a stop to my father's folly," said Atkinson.

"What of the souls within that Realm?" asked Nature.

"They are wasted souls, and are of no use. We cannot put anyone from the Dark Realm back onto the Plane of Existence," observed Dewhirst.

"I am not suggesting you do...but I can put them to good use," mused Nature.

"How so?" asked Atkinson.

"Humans kill indiscriminately and are the only animals to do so; all other animals kill for food, or to protect their brood. These souls could be cleaned and put to use in my Realm. I can turn them into energy – energy that I can use throughout my Realm," suggested Nature.

"Do you want my Warriors to dispatch them to your Realm?" offered Atkinson.

"Yes – but channelled through you, straight to me, is the only safe way of doing it," replied Mother Nature.

"I shall open a channel through my Reaper system straight to you, if that is what you want," said the Scribe, "And I shall do this from now on, whenever I come across an evil soul," he continued.

"Yes. Now that Death is working once more as it is supposed to be, I need to change my direction, and for what I am about to do, I will need as much energy as I can muster," answered Nature.

"What must you do?" queried Atkinson.

"I must show Science that it isn't as bright as the people who work within its boundaries think it is. I will heal the world – not burn it."

With that, Mother Nature bid them farewell and returned to her domain.

Chief Inspector Crawshaw stopped the engine in his car. Stepping outside, he slammed the door closed. Marching into the police station, he bellowed at the desk sergeant, "Bring Paul Johnson to me, now!" Before the police officer could reply, Crawshaw barked, "I didn't say, speak, I said get Johnson!" Turning away, he made his way up to his office. As he sat in his chair, he heard a police car speed away.

I will have answers he thought, as he placed his size nines on the desk.

A police car slowed down to a halt outside the offices of Atkinson, Dewhirst & Smith. Two police officers exited, and entered the building. As ever, the first person they met was Mr. Braithwaite.

"Can I be of assistance, officers?" asked the elderly gentleman.

"We are here to see Paul Johnson," said Officer Harper.

"I shall advise him of your presence," said Mr. Braithwaite as he shuffled away.

Two minutes later, Paul Johnson arrived and said, "Hello, Linda...what seems to be the problem?"

"It's official business, Sir," answered the police officer.

"You don't have to address me as Sir anymore; please come into my office."

Once inside, Johnson offered them a chair. As he sat down at his desk, he said, "How can I help?"

"We have been told to bring you in for questioning," said Linda Harper.

"Really? Questions? And what questions am I to be brought in to answer?" asked Johnson.

"I don't know, Sir, I was just told to bring you in."

"Am I being arrested?"

"No Sir."

"On whose authority am I being brought in?" asked Johnson, as he depressed the button on his two-way radio, asking Braithwaite to bring a tray of tea into his office.

"Chief Inspector Crawshaw, Sir," was the answer from the now unsure police officer.

"Let me get this straight..." at this point, the rattling sound of crockery could be heard as Mr. Braithwaite entered the room. "you are here on Chief Inspector Crawshaw's behalf, passing on his demand that I immediately drop what I'm doing and come to the police station? Would anyone like a spot of tea? Thank you, Mr. Braithwaite, that will be all," said the man who knew a great deal more about situations like this than the two officers sent to implement the order.

"Yes, Sir," said police officer Harper.

"Is that a yes to my question, or to the offer of tea?"

"Uh...the question, Sir."

Johnson sat back, took a sip of his tea, and looked up at the two police officers, saying, "Are we going to discuss the many reasons why I won't be coming back with you...or, do you want to make the mistake of arresting me without due cause?"

The two police officers looked at each other. Not wanting to make such a mistake, police officer Linda Harper said, "I will relay your comments to the Chief Inspector."

"Do please – pass on my regards to him," offered ex-Chief Inspector Paul Johnson.

The two police officers left his office empty-handed.

In the Dark Realm, Dixie was pleased to be united with Gavin and Sarah, as she brought them up to speed on the current situation. This was collectively their first sight of that odious realm.

Its atmosphere was dank, and already, they were feeling down. It wasn't just a feeling of woe, it was as If the whole place was trying to lower their spirits.

"Can you feel that?" asked Dixie.

"Yes, I can," said Gavin, taking his mighty sword from its scabbard.

"I feel it too; we must resist this sadness. Think of something that will make you happy, and once you have that thought, hold onto it," said Sarah.

"What do these Dark Souls look like?" asked Gavin.

"You can't see them – you only know they're there when one touches you. The separate forms of energy are not of interest to us – We have to feel for the two strongest points of energy – one of them will be the Saviour-Child, the other is our target," informed Dixie

"Dixie, I want you to latch onto the stronger power source – that will be the Saviour-Child," said Gavin.

"His name is Paladin," said Dixie.

"I know," said Sarah. "We were at his naming ceremony," she continued. A Slabgirl smile adorned the warrior's face.

"Can you sense the Dark One, Sarah?" asked the Sentinel.

"He is here...he is all around, but most of his energy I sense to be about 3 miles to the Southern end of this strange realm."

"Let's fix upon that position, and leave," said the Sentinel.

"No, we should stay awhile...suddenly I don't feel very much like doing this," said Sarah.

Dixie looked at Gavin, and mouthed the words 'It's this awful place'.

Gavin nodded and turned to Sarah. "It's time to leave here."

"There is too much sadness here! So much pain! I am beginning to feel numb."

"Sarah! Snap out of this! We have work to do!" said Gavin.

Sarah was beginning to change back into human form.

"No!" screamed Dixie. "If she changes back, she'll die!"

Gavin took hold of Sarah by the shoulders and shook her. "Sarah! Sarah! Snap out of this!"

Sarah's eyes began to close, and Gavin slapped her face with the palm of his hand. Sarah's eyes opened instantly, as she changed back into Warrior mode and drew her sword. Faster than a bullet, her sword's point rested at Gavin's throat.

"Now, do I have your attention?" said Gavin. "Just a few seconds ago you were saying, hold onto a pleasant thought. We nearly lost you there. Could you please lower your weapon?"

Sarah took her tearful gaze away from his eyes and saw a trickle of blood begin to drip from the point of her blade. Instantly dropping her sword, she flung her arms round his neck.

"Gavin — I saw awful things! Being engulfed with loathing, I nearly killed you!"

"No amount of despair could make you do that! You hold onto the love we share; nothing within this awful place can fight that!"

Sarah smiled again, and said, "You are right, nothing is stronger than our love! Let's go and find whatever it was that just made that happen, and dispatch it to the four winds!"

"We can't kill it...we have to deliver it to Paladin," informed Dixie.

At the very centre of that odious realm of doom and despair lurked an entity...very dark, very disturbed, and hell-bent on revenge. It knew what it wanted to wreak its revenge upon, but for now, the five intruders within its Realm would be a good start. Like a hunter awaiting its prey, it began to hatch a plan to escape finally — from the tomb that had held it captive within this Realm, for good.

In the Other Realm, Atkinson was feeling uneasy. He sensed something wasn't right. He walked into the Scribe's chambers.

"Atkinson, you are troubled?" said Dewhirst.

"Indeed, I am."

"You have a right to be...what our Warriors are facing, they are facing alone, with diminished powers."

"What's this?"

"The Dark Realm reduces their abilities," said Dewhirst.

"I wasn't aware of this."

"I know."

"If I had known this, I would not have sent them in there!" said Atkinson, clenching his fists

"That is precisely the reason I kept my counsel," said Dewhirst.

"We must bring them out...now!" replied Atkinson.

"Alas...the journey into the Dark Realm is a one-way ticket."

"You have let me send them in there, knowing this?"

"Would you have sent three others? Perhaps yourself, Tamara and I? Is that who you think should have gone?" said Dewhirst.

Atkinson hung his head, saying, "I know we couldn't go. But I could have gone alone; after all, it is my father who initiated that awful place. It should have been me who destroyed it!"

"A fine sentiment indeed, and I agree that you would have been brave enough to attempt such folly. However, it has taken thousands of years to get you ready to take your position, and should you fall – the only one who could take your place is Smith. Now, he is a fine Reaper...there is a touch of destiny about him...but he has had the position for only a small part of this century! He will need countless more centuries before he could face such an undertaking!" said Dewhirst.

"What do I do now? Do I just sit here, and hope that my three Warriors will emerge from that place?"

"Yes. Believe in your actions and trust your Warriors! You must hope, for their sake, that they get whatever lurks within that realm out of there. If not, they have no chance of surviving it."

"We deliver Death. Where is this hope that you speak of? Did you not say that this was a one-way ticket," said Atkinson.

"The way things were when we sent them in, yes it was a one-way ticket...but as we have just learned from Mother Nature herself, you have altered that..." informed Dewhirst. "so, we do not know either way."

At the police station, the two officers arrived back, and Linda Harper went straight to Chief Inspector Crawshaw's office.
"Do you have him in the interview room?" he said.
"No Sir, he wouldn't come with us."
Crawshaw slammed his fists on the desk, overturning his cup and displacing everything upon it, and screamed, "I knew I should have sent a man to do the job right! Get out of here, you incompetent fool!"

Police officer Linda Harper left the room. Walking away, she took out her Dictaphone from the top left-hand pocket of her tunic and switched it off. She smiled, and in a moment of quiet victory, she said, "Gotcha!"
Just after she had placed it back into her pocket, Chief Inspector Crawshaw rushed past her, knocking her to one side. He went straight past the desk sergeant and out of the building. As soon as he left, Tamara appeared in his office, and replaced his incriminating evidence with a folder full of photographs of the Chief Inspector with known villains and naked prostitutes. With the evidence of Atkinson's misdoings under her arm, she returned to Smith's office and awaited the imminent arrival of Chief Inspector Crawshaw.
She didn't have long to wait before a speeding car screeched to a halt outside. The car door slammed, and a commotion in reception followed. Tamara left the office and elegantly walked to the reception area, to find a frail-looking octogenarian physically restraining Chief Inspector Crawshaw.

"Mr. Braithwaite, would you be so kind as to put the Chief Inspector down? I have been expecting him."

"I want to talk to the organ-grinder, not the monkey," growled Crawshaw.

"In that case, carry on Mr. Braithwaite, and do let me know when he has changed his mind," said Tamara, as she ever-so slowly turned and walked back to the office.

The elderly gentleman then grabbed both of Crawshaw's lapels with one shaky hand and lifted him up against the wall again, explaining, "You cannot come in here and demand to see anyone, and I will not tolerate bad manners!"

Chief Inspector Crawshaw could not believe what was happening, and shouted, "I will have this place closed down, and all of you arrested!"

The Sunny Acres mob just glanced up from their work, placed fingers on their lips and in unison whispered, "Shhh…"

"Just let me know, Sir, when you intend to be civil, and I will gladly let you down," said Mr. Braithwaite.

It wasn't too long before Crawshaw realised that this old man could hold him aloft all day, so he said, "Excuse me, will you kindly let me down, please?"

"Of course, Sir. I will advise my superior that you are here."

Again, Tamara came into reception and said, "Now, you silly little man, that wasn't too difficult, was it?"

"Do you know who you are addressing?" gasped Crawshaw.

"The thing is, you sad little policeman, you don't realise whom you are addressing," said Tamara.

"Johnson's secretary, I suppose. Do not worry, I will deal with you soon enough," said Crawshaw.

Tamara smiled, placed her moist lips next to his ear, and whispered, "I am secretary to no man, especially a human male. I am the Listmaker…have you any idea how easy it would be for me to make a mistake, and list the wrong name?" She withdrew and looked straight at him.

"Is that a threat?" stuttered Crawshaw.

"Chief Inspector Crawshaw, I don't threaten people. I am a girl of action. Now, our Mr. Johnson would like to know the whereabouts of his wife-to-be. He thinks you may be able to help him with his enquiries."

"I am here to ask him questions!"

"I don't think so, Chief Inspector. As our surveillance equipment shows, you were the last person to see our sweet little Dixie, as you both got out of your car and ambled into the woods. The very same wood you came running out of not a half hour later...alone...and looking rather dishevelled, as you got back into your vehicle and sped away."

"You cannot have such equipment on public land!" said the Chief Inspector, as beads of sweat popped out around his hairline.

"The 'public land' you refer to is private land, owned by Atkinson, Dewhirst & Smith, Chief Inspector...so, yes, we can. Now if you would like to follow me, Chief Inspector, Mr. Johnson's office is this way. And by the way, our Mr. Smith is at the police station as we speak, listing poor Dixie as a missing person."

Crawshaw suddenly looked ill as he wiped the sweat from his brow and said, "I've just remembered, I've other things to do..." With that, he quickly left the building.

"Oh, very well done, Tamara!" said Paul Johnson, as he slowly clapped his hands.

Tamara took a bow, and said, "Piece of cake," as she shot him a wink. "How long have you been standing there?" she continued.

"Long enough to see that weasel squirm," he replied.

In the Dark Realm, Sarah was now ready to move on with the mission.

"Can you tell what I'm thinking, Sarah?" asked Gavin.

"No...which is strange, don't you think?" replied Sarah.

"I have a feeling our powers aren't working in this realm," said Dixie.

"Well, this might be interesting," quipped Gavin.

"We have a natural power far greater than any other. – we all have a love for one another. The creatures that dwell in this domain harbour hate. Love will be the power that we use in this place," observed Sarah.

"Indeed, you are correct, Sarah. Dixie, keep Paul firmly fixed in your mind all the time you are in this Realm," instructed Gavin.

"That will be very easy – he is always there," said Dixie, with a smile returning to her face.

"Okay, ladies – here is where we split up. Dixie, you have a rendezvous with Paladin. Sarah and I have a date with whatever lies at the centre of this hopeless place, and that is where we will meet up."

With that, Dixie bid her two friends goodbye, and ran off in the direction of Paladin, Juliantrium, and whatever it was that accompanied them. Sarah and Gavin looked at each other, smiled, and charged in the direction of the Beast that was Overlord of this dark and dismal Realm.

Dixie ran through the lifeless surroundings of this desolate place, her mind totally transfixed on the power source directly in front of her. She was very aware that she wasn't alone. It was as if something followed behind her. She stopped and turned, drawing her sword, as something touched her arm. A feeling of dread began to engulf her. She concentrated on her up-and-coming wedding, and the feeling began to diminish until she felt she could break free, swishing her sword across where she thought her attacker was. She continued running, the power source becoming stronger with every step she took.

Sarah and Gavin were experiencing the same thing as Dixie. As each small entity touched them, they would think happy thoughts, and the entity would leave. It was becoming harder to hold these happy thoughts the nearer they came to the Beast, but their resolve was formidable, and they charged forward – ever forward.

Dixie was growing weary. She had a multitude of entities around her, touching every part of her body. The melancholy was overwhelming. She was still moving forward, but she had tears in her eyes, and her running had slowed down to a fast walk. She was beginning to feel lost and abandoned, desperately trying to think of Paul and their wedding. More and more entities latched onto her until, she couldn't walk anymore. An anxiety took over her feelings. Why had Sarah and Gavin left her alone? Were they plotting against her? By sending Dixie in this particular direction, they were keeping the entities away from themselves and leading them to her! She slumped to the ground; the things she was feeling were utter loneliness, depression, and longing. She had given up the chase and now awaited her fate. Something convinced her that the only reason she was there was sacrificial.

"Why would anyone want to sacrifice you?" said a voice from behind her.

"Because I'm surplus to requirements, and they don't need me."

"My Master needs you – that's why he sent me for you."

"Who are you?"

"Turn around and see."

Slowly Dixie turned to see who she was talking to and said, "You are...a horse!"

"I am most certainly not a horse, I am a unicorn! And don't be forgetting that!" said Juliantrium.

"I don't care what you are, I'm staying here."

Juliantrium moved closer to Dixie and brushed against her arm. Instantly, Dixie's mood improved, and she regained her self-composure, as she stood up.

"Thank you, Juliantrium!"

"You are welcome! Now if you would be so kind as to jump up on my back, I will be able to take you to my Master," said the enchanted unicorn.

Dixie threw one leg over the giant beast, nestling swiftly over Juliantrium's back, and away they galloped. As she rode this magnificent animal, more and more of her energy returned.

A smile came to her face as they sped towards Paladin. The strange thing was, her hair just lay calmly upon her shoulders – the forward motion didn't disturb her hair, nor could she feel the wind on her face! She felt the wretched souls hitting her, but this time, they didn't have the same effect. It was as if they were being absorbed and stored. Onward they galloped until they came to an opening. And there, sitting in the middle of what seemed to be a bubble of bright light, was Paladin. He rose and held out his hand. Dixie took hold, and had the most incredible feeling of euphoria. She slid herself off Juliantrium and knelt before him, still holding his hand.

"Milord, thank you for sending Juliantrium; if you hadn't, I fear I would not have survived."

Paladin just smiled and pulled her back into a standing position, and said, "It is ordained that we join the Warriors together, and deliver these wretched creatures to Nature, and so shall it be."

Dixie had heard the words of Gods, and the words of great humans, but never had she hung on words like she had just heard. She stood in complete awe, and didn't know how to reply. She opened her mouth, but words eluded her tongue. She was totally overwhelmed by the greatness and immense feeling of love in his voice.

On the Plane of Existence, a very shaky Chief Inspector Crawshaw had returned to the woods. He had walked back to the place where he and Dixie had entered the Realm of Nature.

He was glad to see there was no dead body on the ground, or sign of a struggle. He moved to the exact spot in the clearing where they went through, holding out his hands in front of him.

Meanwhile, John Smith returned to his office after delivering the report to the police station that his employee was missing. Just after Smith returned, Paul Johnson entered his office.

"Hello Paul, we have Crawshaw on the defensive. It is now up to you to start working on him. By the time this thing is over, I want a dossier so large that no defence will stand a chance."

"This is a job that I will enjoy," said Johnson.

"By the way, I have replaced his evidence with a slightly different kind. It was going to be done by Dixie, but as we know, Dixie's role in this has changed. So I will be messing with his head from now on." said Tamara.

"You have already made a good start," observed Johnson.

Tamara just smiled and said, "I think I will be enjoying myself."

"With this in mind, is there any news of Dixie and the others?" asked Johnson.

"You will know when we know, Paul – as soon as they leave that place, their buttons will reappear on your phone," said Smith.

Johnson looked at his phone, and realised for the first time three names were missing. "Oh, I see," he said.

Back within the Dark Realm, the power sauce that had transfixed Sarah and Gavin drew ever closer. Sarah stopped, and placing her arm across Gavin's body, she brought him to a halt.

"We are close...what we seek waits not fifty yards in front of us," whispered Sarah.

"I feel it," replied Gavin.

At this point, the overwhelming weight of despair was almost unbearable. Bereft of their Immortal power, they were beginning to feel that this wasn't going to be an easy duel. One of the main problems, besides the crippling melancholy, was the fact that their vison reached far beyond the distance of where their assailant lay in wait...making its exact location a complete mystery

"This is impossible!" said Gavin.

"It's not impossible! Look at me, it's not impossible!" shouted Sarah, as she took hold of Gavin.

The Dark Beast seized this opportunity and lunged forward, knocking Gavin out of Sarah's hands. She instantly drew her sword, lashing out at her invisible foe, almost hitting Gavin in the process. Gavin's eyes began to close, and dark rings were now visible around them. Sarah lunged forward, sword outstretched in her right hand, as she took hold of Gavin in her left. She remembered the day he asked her to marry him, and kissed him; while holding the Dark Entity at bay. His eyes opened as she passed him her greatest memory of love through that passionate kiss. Withdrawing her sword, she twirled around, and retreated to a safe distance. Wrapped in Sarah's arms, Gavin's despair began to leave.

"What happened?" asked Gavin.

"That thing had you within its grasp, so I got you back!" answered Sarah.

"How?"

"Like this..." and she planted the longest kiss ever on his lips.

"I like how you do things!" said the Sentinel. "Where is it now?" he continued.

"It's there – right in front of us, about 100 yards away."

"Why doesn't it attack us?" he asked.

"Because for all its power...which I might add is immense...it can't seem to beat us."

"Love is turning out to be a good defence," observed Gavin.

"Yes it is – but the thing is – we aren't hurting it either – we're inflicting no distress upon it," replied Sarah.

As the stand-off ensued, the Dark Beast was recalling all of its strength from its domain. As each separate entity connected to its Master, the Master grew stronger and stronger. It didn't take long before it had recalled every tormented soul, and the very last ounce of its strength, into its being.

Back in the woods, Crawshaw was tentatively feeling for the opening where he and Dixie had fallen through when he last saw her. He knew he had to find her to save his skin. From her vantage point on a branch overhead, Mother Nature observed this vile animal and, thought, *you will do nicely*. She blew a breath of air his way; it encircled him and made time stand still within its perimeter. Once she had him there, she placed a power within him that would act as a beacon, then she opened a portal between him and the Dark Realm right at his fingertips. Mother Nature sat back and waited.

Dixie sat behind Paladin on the back of Juliantrium as they galloped onwards in the direction of Sarah and Gavin. Dixie held tightly onto Paladin's waist as her strength returned.

"The more time I am spending with you Paladin, the stronger I'm feeling."

"I only give peace – what you are feeling is the tortured souls of this place leaving us, for some reason. We are now making progress unhindered," said Paladin.

"Are your powers working in this place?" she asked.

"My powers work everywhere..." informed Paladin.

"Can you see if my friends still live?"

"My mother and father live, but a great force of power is now closing in on them."

"Tell them to run, Paladin! Tell them to get out of there!"

Sarah looked at Gavin, and they both said together, "Run!"

Quickly, they turned and ran back down the gaunt, deathly path that had led them to the Beast. The Beast itself began to follow. They ran as fast and with as much strength as they could muster, but they were losing ground, and as each frantic second passed, the Beast drew closer. As they ran, all thoughts of weddings, kissing and loving were cast aside as the new thought of survival replaced them. Increasingly, their collective mood began to suffer, as the dread of their situation was now fully realised.

Dixie and Paladin were now galloping at full speed upon Juliantrium, in an attempt to assist their friends, but were still far behind.

As they ran, Gavin looked at Sarah, shouting, "We must split up! You go that way, and I will carry on down the original path."

Sarah bore off to the left, and Gavin ran on down the path, followed by the Beast, who was catching up with him all the time. Sarah, out of breath, collapsed on the ground feeling lost, lonely and useless. She somehow knew the Beast would catch Gavin, and her life would be over. Her depression grew, and she decided to succumb to it, and shut her eyes, forcing a lonely teardrop out of her closing eyelid and down her cheek until it fell to the ground.

Dixie suddenly realised they were not following the energy source; they were, in fact, returning to where she had entered that God-forsaken place. She screamed out, "What are you doing? We must help our friends!"

"Where we now go is the only way I can save them." As Paladin's mental link to his parents was fading fast, he felt their life forces grow weaker than ever. He knew they were in a precarious situation, and he would have to take drastic measures to try and help them. The power of the Beast that chased them grew stronger as it honed in on its prey.

Gavin knew that running away was useless; he could now feel the Beast was upon him. He turned and drew his sword. Screaming the love of his life's name, he ran at his marauding foe, which quickly absorbed his body and then carried on, moving forward ever faster. The Dark Realm in its entirety, and the Sentinel now held within this beast, had just one goal, escape and kill.

The very walls of that damned place had now become unstable, and they began imploding towards the running monstrosity, as it raced into the clearing...and then stopped.

Through the portal, it saw the outstretched hand of Chief Inspector Crawshaw, and recognised its host to escape onto the Plane of Existence. The Beast charged at the open portal. At the very second it touched Crawshaw's hand, Juliantrium leaped through the beast, retrieving the Sentinel from its grasp.

The entity screamed in pain, as the goodness of Juliantrium infiltrated it just before it connected with Crawshaw. The Dark Realm began to collapse, as Dixie and Paladin ran to Juliantrium, with Gavin slumped over the unicorn's back. As the Realm was collapsing, Dixie told Paladin and Juliantrium to go through the portal and save Gavin and themselves.

"What about you?" said Juliantrium.

"This was always a one-way ticket for me," said Dixie.

"She still has work to do within this domain, Juliantrium," answered Paladin, as he led the great unicorn through the portal and onto the Plane of Existence, totally bypassing the Realm of Nature.

"Welcome back, child," said Mother Nature from her perch in the tree.

"Mother! It is good to see you again!" smiled Paladin.

"Welcome to the Realm where you will work, Paladin. I have every faith in you."

"Can you help my father? He was engulfed by the Beast that came through before us," asked Paladin.

"This is not my domain – you must take him to Atkinson. You have your Earth Mother's memories, search those memories, and find Atkinson. He will help the Sentinel, and give you the tools you need for your purpose in this Realm. I will wait here until I know that this odious Realm has totally dissolved," said Mother Nature.

As the Dark Realm crumbled about her, Dixie ran to where her fallen comrade lay, being helped more and more as the Realm lost its stability.

In the darkness of her solitude, Sarah opened her eyes. She could sense Dixie, but she could also sense confusion, and instability. She got up on her hands and knees and then slowly rose to her feet. She couldn't make out where she was, and knew she didn't have long before this Realm would be gone, taking her with it. It was then when she heard Dixie running back to her.

"Dixie, is that you?" screamed Sarah.

"Run towards my voice, Sarah...run to me!" Dixie shouted.

Two Warriors whose strength was returning to almost full power met and embraced each other. "Quick, follow – me we have very little time before this place implodes upon itself!"

The two girls ran the fastest their feet had ever carried them within this Realm as its remnants fell about them. The whole realm was beginning to form a vortex behind them as they ran.

The collapsing realm was disappearing into a dot at the centre of a long tunnel. As the two fled, its twirling mass was devouring everything in its path and advancing at great speed. Both Sarah's and Dixie's heels were almost inside the vortex as Dixie shouted, "There's the portal, run faster!"

At the outer edge of the portal, Mother Nature kept her vigil so she would be ready to close it as the vortex approached. She began the enchantment to seal the portal just as the two Warriors burst through at the very last second. Lying on the ground, desperately trying to get their breaths back, they both howled with delight.

"You left it late, children," observed Mother Nature.

"Yes, but we are back, and safe," said Dixie.

"What about Gavin?" asked Sarah.

"He is on his way to Atkinson with Paladin and Juliantrium. Now off you go to him, because here is where the real work begins," said Nature, as she disappeared back into her Realm.

The two girls, now dressed in normal attire, looked at each, other and mouthed, "Real work?"

Dixie and Sarah stood up, took out their phones and depressed Tamara's button, both instantly disappearing and then reappearing in John Smith's office.

"What has happened to Gavin?" asked Sarah.

"He is in the Other Realm with Atkinson as we speak. I think there is someone in the office next door who would like to see you, Dixie," she continued.

Dixie ran out of the office to her waiting fiancé.

Sarah, although worried, lifted her chin. Looking at Tamara with a smile, she said, "She came back and saved me, you know."

"I know she did, I sent her," said Tamara.

"That decision nearly cost you both of us."

"It was worth the gamble to me," said Tamara.

"Would you have sent me back in for Dixie?"

"No," was the instant response.

"It's a good job I wouldn't have waited for the call, then. As of now, Tamara, that girl's status is the same as mine. I owe my life to her bravery," said Sarah, as she depressed the Atkinson button on her phone.

In the Other Realm, Sarah materialised in front of Paladin. "Hello, you are safe!" she said.

"I am, and thanks to your friend Dixie, so are you, I see."

"And the Beast that took Gavin?"

"The Beast, as you so rightly call it, is at large in your Realm," said Dewhirst as he walked into the chamber.

"What of my husband?"

"I see you have no difficulty with the new way of things," retorted Dewhirst.

"What of my husband, Sire?"

"He lives, but part of his awareness has remained with the entity. He will be kept here until such a time that we restore his normal way of thinking."

"Tell me what I need to do, Sire – whatever it is, even if it is to give my life, I will gladly do it to save him."

"Be aware...Crawshaw now has a more intimate knowledge of you, and will know where to find you. With this in mind, you will be used as bait to get this deviant adversary to a place where we can deal with it," informed Dewhirst.

"There will be no need for any sacrifice, Sarah," said Atkinson as he joined the conversation.

"May I see him?"

"In due course my dear; but first, we must dispatch what's left of my father's Dark Realm to Nature. We will be doing this on the Plane of Existence, because that is where the Beast now resides. And, would you believe it, in the body of our friendly Chief Inspector Crawshaw?" said Atkinson.

"Tell me its whereabouts...I will kill it now!" said Sarah.

"No! That would be unacceptable. We can use this to our advantage to get rid of this troublesome Chief Inspector Crawshaw for good. As long as the inhabitants of the Dark Realm dwell within him, we can deal with him on the Plane of Existence. If, however, they separate from him, I will have to bring them into my Realm here. Now, let's go to your husband, my dear," said Atkinson, as he placed his arm around Sarah's shoulders and walked with her to where Gavin Jackson lay in an induced coma.

Sarah ran and threw her arms around her him. With tears streaming down her soft, pale cheeks, she whispered, "Again you have saved me...now I will save you." Sarah turned to Atkinson and said, "I take it Tamara has a plan of action?"

"Indeed, she does," replied Atkinson.

"In that case, I beg your leave, Sire. I have work to do." With that, Sarah depressed the button marked 'Tamara' on her phone, and was gone.

JOHN PAUL BERNETT

Chapter Ten

The rain pelted against the office windows of the Reaper in Administration. John Smith looked out onto an unusually overcast morning, the image made opaque by the condensation built up upon the window pane.

"Uncommonly miserable weather for summer, isn't it Tamara?" he said.

"There is unrest in the streets, too," was her answer as Sarah materialised in front of her desk.

"Sister! I have been expecting you!"

"How do you want me to slay Crawshaw?" asked Sarah.

"Were you not listening to Atkinson, Sarah? There will be no killing...not yet!"

"Am I to just sit back and wait as my husband worsens and dies while whatever that thing is inside Crawshaw lives?"

"That 'thing', as you call it, is going to help heal this planet. We have to find a way of dispatching it via Mr. Smith from the Realm of Death onto the Realm of Nature. We cannot do that if you run to Crawshaw and relieve him of his head with your sword, now, can we?"

"What will you have me do?" lamented Sarah, lowering her head as tears welled up again.

"Save your tears, for a start...do you think Atkinson would let his beloved Sentinel die?"

"He sent him on a one-way journey!"

"No, Sarah, he wasn't aware of that piece of information until it was too late and the pair of you were already in there."

Sarah looked up and said, "Would he have sent Dixie alone?"

"No, my sweet sister, Atkinson would have ignored the rules set out for such a problem as this and gone in with her himself."

"Why is Dixie so expendable to him?" asked Sarah.

"We are all expendable as long as replacements are available. Smith wasn't ready to take Atkinson's place as figurehead, and Dixie, as yet, isn't prepared to take mine. It comes down to efficacy, not loyalty," was Tamara's hard-hitting answer.

"Now girls, shall we lighten this situation a tad by taking tea? I think we all need to calm down," said John Smith, turning from the window to his desk.

It wasn't long before the quivering crockery arrived and was placed on the table at the side of the room.

"Will there be anything else, Sir?" asked Mr. Braithwaite.

"No, my fine fellow, that will be all," said Smith. "All this will be over within a day or two, and everything will work out fine in the end. Now, who would like a cup of tea?"

Over a cup of perfectly-brewed Darjeeling, Tamara informed Sarah of Mother Nature's plan to recycle the Dark Realm into energy. She also explained how difficult such an undertaking would be.

"Where does Paladin fit into this plan?" asked Sarah.

"That, I'm afraid, I'm not aware of yet," said Tamara.

"Clearly, he's here for some purpose," said Sarah.

"Indeed he is, but I don't think this is it. I think Paladin has to do with the long-term future of this planet, and through him, Nature will work her magic on the Plane of Existence once she has the extra energy from the souls who resided in the Dark Realm," said Smith.

The discussion carried on through the morning and into the afternoon.

As the conversation was taking place, at the other side of the office wall, there was a different type of discussion.

"I was so worried about you! It was hard to think of anything but you," said an elated Johnson.

"I am back now, and hope I never leave your arms again!" replied Dixie as she kissed him on the neck.

"Mmm...that's nice. But what if someone comes in?" said the cautious ex-Chief Inspector.

"I locked the door as I entered," she said, removing his jacket and tie.

In the Other Realm, Dewhirst said to Atkinson, "Let's bring Dixie in, I want to hear what happened in there."

Atkinson hovered his finger over the button marked 'Dixie'. He then smiled and said, "It can wait for an hour or two, Dewhirst."

Chief Inspector Crawshaw was still in the woods, sitting on a stone protruding out of the ground. He was now sporting a rough-looking beard, and bore a demented look on his face. What was left of his mind was in turmoil. The more the Dark Beast within him grew accustomed to its new domain, the worse Crawshaw looked. He lifted his head, and through dimmed eyes he saw what could only be an elder fairy. This fairy was like no picture of one he had ever seen; so much so, she towered above him in height. The fairy then spoke.

"I speak to the Collective Souls within you. I am the one who allowed passage for you into this Realm. I now offer you safe passage as cleansed spirits into my Realm."

"Fuck off, bitch," growled Crawshaw.

"Then you give me no choice but to leave you to Atkinson, and your demise."

"Atkinson? What know you of this name?"

"I know the bearer of that name will hunt you down."

"I will look forward to meeting him again," said Crawshaw as he slunk away.

"You will find this one even stronger than the Creator you seek," answered Mother Nature, as once again she left the Plane of Existence to prepare in her Realm of Nature the future of Humankind.

The Dark Beast, Crawshaw, continued walking towards the car. All along the path that Crawshaw had trod, the vegetation withered and died. The day had become dark and cold; there was little birdsong to be heard. Misery now followed in his wake, as he shuffled into the car, and sped away. Within minutes, he was back at the police station.

Desk Sergeant Glenn Simpson called to him as he walked in. Crawshaw walked up to the police officer and grabbed him by the lapels of his tunic, pulling him over the desktop. Crawshaw looked at the bewildered Sergeant, and hit him across the face with the back of his hand, knocking him to the ground.

"Do not disturb me! Any of you, understand?" snarled Crawshaw as he climbed the stairs to his office.

Once inside, he sat in the chair and looked about the room. The Dark Beast within him realised the irony of his host. A large number of the souls within Crawshaw had been placed into the Dark Realm via the hangman's noose or the electric chair – put into that situation by the police – just like the one his Dark Army now infested.

Downstairs, having stood up and adjusted his uniform, Police Sergeant Glenn Simpson took up his position back behind the front desk. Looking at the stunned police officers around him, he asked, "Are any of you prepared to say you witnessed what has just taken place?"

There was an awkward silence for a moment, but it was broken by police officer Linda Harper, who pushed forward through the other officers and said, "I witnessed it – and furthermore, I want to make an official complaint about harassment and sexual discrimination from my superior, Sarge!"

After police officer Harper broke the ice, the rest of the assembled officers agreed to be witness to Crawshaw's appalling behaviour.

"This isn't going to go well for him, because earlier I had John Smith in here, reporting one of his staff as a missing person. The last time she was seen was when she entered the woods with the Chief Inspector...but he came out alone. I have just sent the report to HQ," said Police Sergeant Glenn Simpson.
"You don't think he...?"

Police officer Linda Harper was stopped by Sergeant Simpson saying, "I have just reported the facts to my superiors as reported to me. There was surveillance equipment footage showing the employee and the Chief Inspector both going in, and only Chief Inspector Crawshaw leaving," interrupted the Sergeant.

As the police officers were making their separate statements, the phone at the front desk rang. Police Sergeant Simpson answered. It was the phone call he had been waiting for, and the official on the other end of the line told him to expect a visit, and to limit the Chief Inspector's movements until she arrived.

The day moved on, and Atkinson finally summoned Dixie into his realm. As she arrived, she knelt down down before him.

"Rise, Dixie – there is no need for you to kneel when summoned. First and foremost, you are no longer an unimportant elemental. Secondly, after your exploits in the Dark Realm, I should kneel to you."
"I was just doing your bidding, Sire."
"Dixie, please stand up, I want to talk with you."

Nervously she stood, looked at Atkinson and gave him a small smile.

"That's better, my dear. Now, tell me about the power of this Beast we chase."

"I'm sure the Sentinel or the Earth Mother can inform you better than I, Sire."

"No Dixie, they cannot. The Sentinel is unconscious. The Earth Mother only speaks of killing said Beast – a practice, I have found to my peril twice, that she is quite adept at performing. You were with Paladin, so through him, you will have gained some idea of what we fight."

"Well, Sire, our telepathic capabilities were limited in that realm."

"Yes, but they were stronger than Sarah and Gavin's," replied Atkinson.

"He is formidable...hate fuels him, and he seeks the Creator."

"Excellent! That will guide him straight to me! I think it's time you and John Smith had a small holiday."

"But what of Paul? Can he come too?"

"I'm afraid not, we need him here, because we fight this Beast on two levels. By the way, you, my dear, are a missing person – and that is very useful to me at this time. Now, go and say your goodbyes." With that, she was back in Paul Johnson's office.

"I have to go away," frowned Dixie.

"I know; I was summoned to Dewhirst whilst you went to Atkinson."

"Did Dewhirst say for how long?" asked Dixie.

"It will be until Atkinson and Tamara sort out the reaping of this thing from the Dark Realm; a couple of days, no more," was Johnson's reply.

Back in the Other Realm, Dewhirst questioned Atkinson's actions.

"Two things puzzle me, Atkinson; firstly, why do you and Tamara need to perform this task? Secondly, why take the girl out of the equation?"

"The reason it has to be me and not Smith is because I have only now realised his potential, so it would not be a good time to lose him. As for Dixie, one of the Dark Realm's occupants has already shared her thoughts. Potentially, that could be dangerous, as she could give away – albeit unknowingly – our proceedings. And for the record – it should have been my Administration."

These answers were accepted by Dewhirst, as he said, "Agreed; I have instructed Johnson as to what transpired here."

"Very well, begin the process of replacement. I will go and explain to the people in the office. I will see you when things are back to normal," said Atkinson.

"Is this how it will always be?" asked Dewhirst.

"How what will be?"

"You, taking over whenever there is trouble."

"Only for the next millennia," answered Atkinson, his eyes showing a glint of excitement.

"Do remember, this time, the first three days you are vulnerable. Also, it would be wise to remember that to the people on that plane you, my friend, are dead," instructed Dewhirst as the smiling Atkinson disappeared.

He reappeared in front of Smith. Still smiling, he said, "I am back as Reaper for a while."

John Smith placed his finger on the intercom button and asked Mr. Braithwaite to come in. Within seconds, Mr. Braithwaite had joined the gathered ensemble.

"Mr. Braithwaite, there is to be a change of Reaper."

"I am afraid I can't allow that, Sir, the bookkeeping would be erroneous, and that cannot occur," explained the old gentleman.

"Tis but a brief change, Mr. Braithwaite; we have to do things a little different for a day or two. I will reap on this plane, whilst Mr. Smith has a little break in the Realm of Death."

"I don't quite follow, Sir," said Braithwaite.

"You don't follow because what we do is a brand-new concept, Mr. Braithwaite. What will transpire is a one-off between ourselves, and the Goddess of Nature."

"That is most irregular, Mr. Atkinson. May I use a different ledger for your time with us so as not to disrupt the regular goings on?"

"I would welcome that very thing, Mr. Braithwaite!" agreed Atkinson, as the satisfied elderly gentleman left the office.

"Bureaucrats! Crossing the T's and dotting the I's! However, he is right – this has never been done before," said Atkinson.

"What is it we are doing?" enquired Smith.

"Nature tried to get Crawshaw to go straight into her Realm from the Plain of Existence, but all she is allowed to do from this Realm is ask. Of course, Crawshaw refused. We have to get what is inside of him from him. We then have to dispatch them from within Crawshaw to someone who is on Tamara's list; that's where you come in, Smith. You will be ready in the Realm of Death, awaiting this person's mortal cord to appear. When the cord appears, you will cut it, thus releasing said souls into the nearest object – which, if all has gone to plan, will be me."

"I take it that it will not be as simple as you've just made it sound," said Tamara.

"There may be problems, if they don't all cross over to me," answered Atkinson. "If that happens, we will all be called into action. All, that is, except Dixie. Dixie is going away, as she must remain on the missing person's list, because when we reap the souls to Nature, we are still left with this troublesome Chief Inspector."

"We can take care of him when this is done...but what about Gavin?" asked Sarah.

"Should our plan prevail, as soon as the souls pass into Nature, we will pull him out of his coma."

"But I thought..."

Atkinson interrupted Sarah by saying, "Gavin is in a coma for his protection. The Beast has a link with him – that's all. That link would give my adversary an unfair advantage, so I have removed it."

"When does all this begin?" asked John Smith.

"In three days' time. As Tamara will point out to you, John, if for any reason you come back to the Plane of Existence to start an Administration before your time, you are vulnerable for the first three days."

Tamara hung on his words, thinking back to the turn of the 21stcentury, and Sarah plunging that blade deep into his temple. That image diminished as Dixie and Paul Johnson entered the room, bringing her out of her daydream.

"Welcome, Dixie and Paul – perfect timing! While Sarah and I deal with Crawshaw, John will be in the Realm of Death, waiting for the call, and Tamara will also be awaiting our call in the office. You, Dixie, will be in hiding...anywhere you desire to go, it is up to you. This will help Paul's case against the Chief Inspector. The case Paul will be working on will be a murder investigation, and Dixie will be the one who has supposedly been murdered," said Atkinson.

Paul Johnson nodded his approval.

Dixie entered the discussion by saying, "You say I can go anywhere I like?"

"Just name the place, and in three days' time you will be there," answered Atkinson.

"In that case, I should like to spend my time off in your Realm, Sire."

"My Realm, Dixie?"

"Yes, Gavin Jackson – is there, and the one thing I know about this thing we chased is, it is very powerful. So I will defend the Sentinel."

"Dewhirst will be doing that very thing," answered Atkinson.

"I understand that, Sire, but if I am there, Mr. Dewhirst is at your disposal should you need him on this Plane," said Dixie.

Atkinson looked at Dixie, and unlike his father, who would have instantly killed her for insolence – thinking she could advise him on a decision – he smiled, and said, "Let this be a lesson to all in this room. If you ever have a better idea than mine, speak up! Dixie, that is an excellent idea, thank you!"

Dixie couldn't believe that not only was she living with these beings, but the Great God Atkinson had spoken to her and also praised her! She bowed her head, and remembered how insignificant she had been until Tamara pointed a finger at her in the Other Realm, and said, *You! Step forward! Guard the human named Paul Johnson with your life, and make sure that everything he desires is granted!*

"As far as I'm concerned, we all convene again in three days' time. As for now, I think a trip to Wednesday's Wardrobe is in order! When did I last buy you a dress, Tamara?"

Tamara smiled and said, "I'm too busy thinking about the one you're going to buy me now to remember any in the past, my love."

"Paul, your investigation will be hard work, so I have decided to give Dixie and yourself three days away. There is a tropical island in the Other Realm whose only inhabitants are my personal elementals. I'm sure you two will love it!" said Atkinson, as he closed his eyes. Instantly Dixie and Paul Johnson were gone.

"What of Paladin, while all this is going on? Surely he can be of assistance in all of this?" asked Sarah.

"I'm still not sure...I think Mother Nature will call upon his powers when we reach the point where she's accepting the souls from the Dark Realm. But as I have said, his powers are different to ours. I am sure Paladin's future lies in the saving of the planet," said Atkinson.

At the other end of town, Crawshaw lifted the receiver on his phone and called down to the Desk Sergeant.

"Can I be of assistance, Sir?" asked Sergeant Glenn Simpson.
"Send me two of your people up, now!"

Glenn Simpson put the phone down just as an official-looking woman entered the police station.

"Do excuse me one moment, Ma'am…" said Glenn Simpson as he told two police officers to go up to the Chief Inspector's office.

"Delay that request," said the woman.

"Thank you very much for your speedy response, Detective Superintendent Malik," said Glenn Simpson.

"Where is Chief Inspector Crawshaw?" she continued.

"The Chief Inspector is in his office, ma'am, I will let him know you are here."

"No, Sergeant Simpson, where is his office? I will see him unannounced."

The Sergeant asked one of his officers to escort the Superintendent to Crawshaw's office. He then turned back to Superintendent Malik, saying, "The Chief Inspector is behaving in an odd fashion, ma'am, it might be a good idea to have an officer in the room with you."

"Thank you, Sergeant, but I don't think that should be necessary at this point…although depending on the interview, that may change."

"As you wish, ma'am, but I would like the officer to escort you inside, and if you feel secure, he will leave."

There was a tap on Crawshaw's door and the superior officer walked in unannounced. The unwashed, unshaven Crawshaw looked up, expecting two police officers. Under the influence of the Dark Realm, he could not distinguish the two in front of him being anything different than that. One thing he did notice was that one of them was female. He picked up his phone without taking his deadpan gaze from the two people in front of him.

"Why do you keep sending me women, you idiot!" he screamed into the phone.

"I beg your pardon!" said his superior.

"Deaf as well as stupid, are you? Get out of here!" growled Crawshaw.

"This interview is over, Chief Inspector Crawshaw. Hand over your Warrant Card. I am suspending you until further notice," said a shocked Malik.

"Get out of my office, or I will throw you out!" snarled Crawshaw.

"Oh you will, will you? You are in enough trouble already. Give me your badge...now!" With that, Crawshaw rose up from his chair and moved towards the Detective Superintendent. The other police officer stood himself between his two superior officers to offer protection to Viktoria Malik, but his Chief Inspector took hold of him, and with ease threw him against the wall, rendering him unconscious. The Detective Superintendent couldn't believe her eyes as Crawshaw grabbed hold of her by her arms and leaned forward, his face almost touching hers. He put his nose right up to her face, and began to take in her perfume, sniffing like a dog. He grinned, showing stained teeth, releasing his gut-wrenchingly strong bad breath. Malik felt sick to her stomach but resisted his advance. She sunk her pointy shoe deep into his groin. He instantly let go of her arm, and she quickly made her escape. Crawshaw regained his composure and followed his superior officer out of the room. As she ran down the stairs, the officers in attendance ran to her assistance. Malik screamed at Simpson, "Get back up, he's out of control!"

Glenn Simpson immediately switched on his radio, asking all officers within the vicinity to return to the police station, quick-smart.

Crawshaw burst around the corner at the top of the stairs, and once again made for Detective Superintendent Malik. As the small number of officers advanced towards him, he repelled each and every one of them. As they tried to restrain the now totally out of control Crawshaw, Glenn Simpson took hold of his superior Officer's hand, and ran out of the door with her.

A police car screeched to a halt outside with its blue lights flashing and siren blaring. Sergeant Glenn Simpson opened the back door and forcibly placed Viktoria Malik on the back seat, then screamed at police officer Linda Harper to drive off. She put her foot down hard on the accelerator, and the police car sped away.

Glenn Simpson then turned and ran back inside, along with the other officers answering his distress call. Once inside, they joined the fray, as one officer after another received a beating and unceremoniously smashed into the walls by this beast of a man who had become completely deranged. It didn't take very long for there to be twenty-two police officers – men and women of all ranks up to detective – laid to waste on the floor, with broken bones, lacerations, and for officers Edwards and Thomas – broken necks. The Beast just strode over the carnage and into the outside world, taking with him the body of Crawshaw, as it needed his life force to survive on the Plane of Existence. Glenn Simpson just about managed to call for an ambulance as he passed out.

The police car that had Viktoria Malik as a backseat passenger pulled to a halt in the car park of a local supermarket. Police officer Linda Harper turned around from her driving position and said, "Can you tell me what's going on, please?"

"What is your name?" inquired her superior officer in plain clothes.

"Police Officer Harper; now, can you please tell me what's happened? I received a call to hurry back to the station, and my Sarge threw you into the back of my car!"

"First of all, I am Detective Superintendent Viktoria Malik; for your report, that is Viktoria with a K, not a C. Your 'Sarge' has just saved my life, quite possibly at the cost of his own. The Chief Inspector is quite deranged, and needs to be arrested at the earliest possible opportunity. Now take me to Central Headquarters, please."

"Excuse me, ma'am, but I need to return to help my comrades."

"Harper, there is nothing you can do there. Pass me your radio, and patch me through to HQ."

Linda Harper handed Viktoria Malik her radio, and the Detective Superintendent advised the central police station for the city to get as many people over as possible to Chief Inspector Crawshaw's station. Police Officer Linda Harper drove the Superintendent back to her HQ. As she pulled up, Viktoria Malik asked her to follow her inside. Both women walked straight through Reception to the Detective Superintendent's office. Taking her jacket off, Malik asked Harper to sit down.

"Now…Linda, let's dispense with rank. Before we start officially, tell me all you know about this Chief Inspector Crawshaw. You can call me Viktoria."

At the other police station, reinforcements had arrived. The ambulances and medics were already in attendance, administering relief to the wounded officers. The official in charge was Detective Sergeant Craig Walsh, who was in conversation with Sergeant Glenn Simpson. He was taking a statement from him, and asked, "Are you the sergeant who placed a complaint against Crawshaw this morning?"

"I am," confirmed Simpson.

"What happened here?"

"Detective Superintendent Malik arrived, and asked to be led upstairs unannounced."

"And then what?"

"And then, not long after, she came running down the stairs quite distressed, being chased by Chief Inspector Crawshaw."

"Did he cause all this devastation?"

"Yes."

"According to my reports from different officers, more than twenty of you were overcome…are you trying to tell me it was by Crawshaw?"

"He was like an animal," stated Glenn Simpson.

"Animal or not, I find it hard to believe one man did all this."

"The CCTV is still running, Sir, you might want to check it for yourself."

"Don't get an attitude with me, Sergeant."

"Don't get an attitude!" said the Desk Sergeant, as he struggled to get to his feet, and pointed to the two dead police officers in the corner of the room. "Don't get an attitude!? Two of my officers are dead, and you don't believe what I'm saying?! Check the recording, Sir!" he insisted, as he turned his back on D.S. Walsh and walked over to his slain comrades.

Back at police HQ, the conversation between Detective Superintendent Viktoria Malik and Police Officer Linda Harper was carrying on, still off the record.

"Tell me about Crawshaw, Linda."

"He's a sexist pig."

"You sound like you have personal experience of this."

"I have, ma'am."

"Call me Viktoria...this is off the record. I have to get my thoughts together about this man before I go on the record, Linda."

The smile from Viktoria Malik made Linda Harper feel more at ease.

"Well...Viktoria, he has made sexist remarks to me in all my dealings with him. He always complains about women officers, and how they aren't capable of doing their jobs. He is violent, too – he dragged Sergeant Simpson over the front desk, and slapped him across his face with the back of his hand, knocking him to the ground."

"Did you witness this attack on Simpson?"

"I did – and several other officers witnessed it also, all of whom have now submitted a report on the assault."

"It isn't looking good for Chief Inspector Crawshaw...and there is a missing person, as well...with him being the last one seen with her," said Viktoria.

There was a knock on the door, and Malik shouted, "Enter!"

"There has been a terrible occurrence at the police station on Park Road, ma'am," said Police Sergeant Morris."

"That's where I've just come from!" said the superintendent.

"I know, ma'am – we sent people there, but we were too late," said the sergeant.

"What do you mean, too late?" asked Linda Harper.

"There are more than twenty injured...and I'm afraid two are dead."

"Dead?!" shouted Linda. "Ma'am...I need to get back!" she continued.

"Of course...I will come with you," said Viktoria, placing her jacket back over her shoulders.

The two women left police HQ and headed towards Park Road Police Station. When they arrived, the whole area was cordoned off by the police. Getting out of the car, Malik showed her Warrant Card to the officer on duty, and walked into the building with Linda Harper.

There was blood everywhere, but most of the injured were already in the hospital. The two dead police officers, however, were being photographed by the forensic team. Burke and Hare were ready with their body bags, but there was no sign of the pathologist.

"Where is Dr. Jackson?" asked Viktoria Malik.

"He...he can't be found, ma'am...his assistant is on his way," said Glenn Simpson.

"I don't want an assistant!"

"He is a qualified Pathologist ma'am, and works very closely with Gavin Jackson," assured Simpson.

"Okay, thank you. By the way, Sergeant Simpson, if it hadn't been for your quick thinking, I might have been getting photographed along with these two unfortunate officers."

"Three," corrected Simpson.

"How so?"

"There is another dead police officer in Crawshaw's office...he was the one who took you up earlier," said Simpson.

"This is unreal...what has happened here, Sarge?" gaped Linda Harper.

"Carnage...carnage from a madman," answered Simpson.

"Are you alright, Sarge?" she asked.

"I would be if that idiot in the suit would stop asking me stupid questions."

Viktoria Malik looked up and shouted, "Detective Sergeant Walsh!"

Walsh came over to where she was standing.

"I'm in charge now, Detective Sergeant...you can stand down and go back to your office."

Detective Sergeant Walsh replied, "Yes ma'am," and left.

"There, Sergeant Simpson. I know I was here, but can you can tell me from your perspective what happened?"

"I can do better than that, ma'am, I can show you if you would like to come with me...I have it all on CCTV."

"Excellent! Lead on," said Malik.

Police officer Linda Harper walked over to where the two dead officers were lying, trying to hold back her tears.

As the CCTV footage was replaying the incident for the Superintendent, Tom Harper arrived at the scene of the crime.

"Over here, Sir!" said one of the police officers.

Tom Harper made his way to the first of the two bodies. It wasn't long before the cause of death was noted, and the bodies removed.

"Where is Dr. Jackson?" queried Malik as she returned from viewing the CCTV footage.

"He is unwell, so I must do this in his stead," answered the very polite Tom Harper. "They both died from a broken neck sustained by a single blow. Of course, I won't be fully able to confirm that until the autopsies."

"I can confirm that for you – I've just watched it happen on CCTV. You will, however, be able to tell me what strength that hand must have had to inflict the deaths of these two and the one upstairs so easily."

"Everything will all be in my report, Vik...uh, sorry, Chief Superintendent."

Viktoria Malik gave Tom Harper a knowing glance over the top of her spectacles and said, "How soon, Tom...uh, sorry, Dr. Harper?"

He smiled and said, "Quasimogirl is also unwell, so with no distractions, it will be on your desk tomorrow morning."

As Tom made his way upstairs to the third body, he passed Linda Harper. He put his forefinger under her chin and gently lifted it, giving her a smile. Viktoria also moved over to where Linda stood. She noticed she was looking very distressed, and said, "Now, my dear...don't take this to heart...you are a police officer, and our kind of officers have to work that little bit harder to hold our emotions in because of people like Crawshaw – if you know what I mean."

Linda Harper nodded and said, "Thank you, ma'am. If you don't mind me asking, how do you know Tom?"

"Normally, I would be very angry about such a question."

"I'm sorry, ma'am, I was out of line."

"Let me finish, Officer Harper...come with me, there is no more I can do here. We can have a chat."

"Of course, ma'am," was the obedient reply.

The two women left the building as Tom Harper recorded his thoughts on the third body, removed his gloves, and said his goodbyes. Outside the police station, the three people met up again, as Tom Harper walked over to where they were standing.

"Right – I will be off, then," said Tom.

"I'm going to have to come and see you at work...'Quasimogirl' indeed," laughed Viktoria!

"Keep away, for the sake of your sanity!" said Tom, as he kissed Linda Harper gently on her cheek and made his way to the car.

"I know Tom because we move in certain circles. We have...things in common, let's say. Alas, you seem to know him better than I do...but I must say that I am quite surprised," said Malik disappointedly.

Linda Harper let out a small giggle and said, "Oh no, ma'am, it's nothing like that – he is my brother!"

Detective Superintendent Viktoria Malik smiled and said, "Oh, I see! But, I'm sure a beautiful girl like you has lots of admirers..."

Linda Harper just lowered her head and said, "Um...I...err..."

"It's okay, Linda, I understand the discrimination that goes on when people don't fit exactly into the mould."

"Thank you for understanding, ma'am. I think it would halt my progress if people knew I was, shall we say, different."

"It didn't hamper my progress," informed Malik.

Linda Harper's eyes widened as she said, "You're...I mean, are you, uh..."

Malik's interjection helped Harper's search for the right words to say, "A lesbian?" she whispered. "Yes Linda, I am, now another question – and please forgive its forthrightness – do you have a girlfriend?"

Linda Harper just shook her head and said, "No."

"In that case, your work for the day has ended. Go home and have a rest. Try to forget about what's happened here today and maybe, if you feel up to it that is, we could have a spot of dinner tonight, my treat."

"Is that an order, ma'am?"

"No, Linda, it's a request. A strange one to make at a murder scene, I know, but a request nonetheless."

"Then I accept, Viktoria."

"My close friends call me Vik. Come on, I will drop you off at home, and I will return at eight."

The two new friends sat in the car and drove off with thoughts of that night's meeting replacing thoughts of murder.

Crawshaw had wandered aimlessly after he left the police station. He began to feel tired, so he sat down under Crown Point Bridge to the South side of the river, his mind now totally under the influence of the Dark Realm. Any traces of the police officer had vanished. All he felt now was hate, and all he sought was revenge. The only word in his head was 'Atkinson'. All he wanted to do was kill. Standing up, he placed himself aloft in the Victorian girders of the bridge, and formulated his plans to destroy everything that Atkinson stood for, and all who stood in his way. He lay back on the girder, out of sight of the passing strollers, cyclists and dog-walkers, and fell into a deep, rejuvenating sleep.

Chapter Eleven

ixie and Paul Johnson found themselves lying on the pure white sands of a tropical paradise. They both sat up and looked around the place. A more beautiful, idyllic part of the world could not exist. Paul Johnson looked at Dixie and said, "Have you ever seen a sky so blue?"

"Only for other people," answered Dixie.

"Come on, let's explore," urged Paul.

They both rose and started walking along the sand. To the side of the beach was a luxurious house that begged to be investigated. Paul slid the large glass door open effortlessly, and they both entered. Dixie sunk into one of the couches. As soon as she did, an elemental appeared, with a bottle of Boerl & Kroff Brut Champagne.

"Wow, just look at that! That stuff is about £1,500.00 a bottle!" gasped Johnson.

"How do you know that? I thought you were a beer man!" said Dixie.

"Oh, I am, the bubbles of champagne get right up my nose. I was attending a burglary investigation with Chief Inspector Thompson once, and a case of that particular sparkling wine had been reported stolen. I couldn't believe it when the woman whose wine it was told me its value."

"Come and sit next to me – we have three days of pampering ahead of us, and I, for one, am going to enjoy it," said Dixie.

"Me too," said Paul Johnson, joining her on the couch.

In the Other Realm, Sarah sat at the side of Gavin Jackson, holding his hand, when Atkinson walked in the room.

"It's no use trying to contact him, Sarah; I have made it so that the only contact with him must pass through me, and that's how it must stay."

"Why have you done that?" she asked.

"The reason I am doing that is if anyone is trying to connect with him, they have to do it through me, thus, giving away their position – and who they are."

"I see," said Sarah.

"He knows of the situation, but most of all he knows he is safe here. He is missing on the Plane of Existence, so I need you to smooth things over back there until we get this problem sorted. We don't want Gavin disappearing now as well as Dixie, do we?"

"I understand, although it will be hard to not be sad back there."

"No, it won't, Sarah. You will be your usual self, because as far as anyone will be concerned, you have him at home with the flu. Whenever you are in that realm, you have a choice between the un-bested warrior that you are, or the scatter-brained, annoying little Slabgirl. When you return there, you can hardly parade around with a pair of wings, wearing armour and standing two to three feet taller than most people, now, can you?"

"I suppose not," she said with a smile.

"Begone then, Gorezilla," laughed Atkinson.

"To think...your father tried to kill her," said Dewhirst as Sarah departed.

"As did I – it's a good job you sired strong offspring, Dewhirst, a good job indeed," smiled Atkinson.

Sarah arrived back at the Pathology lab just as Burke and Hare were delivering the three police officers, closely followed by Tom Harper.

"Hello there, strange young thing! I have a good memory for faces, and I seem to know yours...have we worked together before, perhaps?"

"Hello, Tommy...what's happened here, then?"

"I have had to go to the police station as some deranged police officer has killed these poor individuals and injured twenty others. Do you know why I had to leave this wonderful place of solitude, and go myself?"

"Oh...I know this one, it's because Gavin isn't here, isn't it?"

"Well, it isn't because you were missing. What have you done with him, you nasty girl?"

"Nothing, he has a severe case of man-flu."

"Hmm...yes, you are apparently wearing the poor man's immune system down."

"I never touch his CD equipment, only old people use them. I have an MP3 Player."

"Good for you! MP3 player indeed...now put the kettle on and make some tea. With there only being two of us, you are going to have to do some work today. And you two!" shouted Tom Harper, "Have a little respect for the dead when you bring them here!"

Burke and Hare just looked at him, showing absolutely no emotion as they left their deliveries and walked out.

"Talk about fitting the job you are doing...those two are without doubt the strangest people I have ever met!" said Tom.

Looking at Sarah as she returned with the tea, he said. "I take that back..."

"You take what back, Tommy?"

"Nevermind."

The day went by quickly; just as the clock was chiming eight, Linda Harper's front door bell rang. She hesitated a moment, thinking...*What you are doing!*? But then, the thought of *how a superintendent dresses when she is off-duty* kicked in, so she ran to the door. As she opened it, she couldn't believe her eyes. The most senior officer that had ever spoken to her was standing in front of her wearing a long black dress with stiletto-heeled shoes. Her hair was down and over her shoulders, and she was wearing makeup! She was not what Linda had expected at all!

"Do you approve?" asked Viktoria Malik, doing a little twirl on the steps.

"I...I am...wow! Please come in, where are my manners? You look beautiful!"

"As do you, Linda."

"No, I look...uh...please, sit down. I will only be a couple of minutes," said Linda, as she ran back up the stairs.

Viktoria sat down in the living room, wondering what was wrong. Her dinner guest looked like she was ready – dressed sedately – but ready. A few minutes passed, and Linda Harper returned to the living room. This time, the word 'sedate' was forgotten. She was wearing a long black skirt with black mesh over the fabric, a pair of stiletto-heeled New Rock boots, and a black mesh slightly see-through top that was figure-hugging, showing a glimpse of a leopard-skin-patterned bra. She too had let her hair down, and it fell just onto her shoulders.

"Linda – just look at you! You are gorgeous!" exclaimed Viktoria.

"You approve, then?"

"I love it! I wish I'd have put my New Rocks on now."

"I can't believe we like the same clothing...where do you shop?" queried Linda.

"Wednesday's Wardrobe, in the Merrion Centre."

"Me too! But I've never seen you in there before..."

"Would you have recognised me? Because I certainly wouldn't have recognised you," said Viktoria.

"I suppose not; I do love that shop!" enthused Linda.

"I know Wednesday, she is a friend of mine. I will introduce you properly to her, if you would like," said Viktoria.

"That would be great! I would love to look like her – she has a particular style that most can't pull off. I'm so glad that you and I share the same style of dress!"

"I love it – especially the splash of leopard skin."

Linda smiled and said, "There may be more than just a splash."

Viktoria smiled and said, "I'd better make sure this night goes well then, hadn't I? Because as I've already mentioned, I do love leopard skin."

At the offices of Atkinson, Dewhirst & Smith, Tamara gave John Smith his list. He glanced through it and said, "It's an odd job that I do."

"It isn't the usual 9 to 5, but it has perks, and much better long-term prospects than any other job. Speaking of the perks, what news of Tom Harper?"

"We have a lot in common! I say a lot, because, we both work with Death, and apparently we are both gay."

"What more do you need? Sounds like a perfect match! There will be more to it than that though, John...there is the physical aspect, as well."

"I know...the problem with that is, I think Tom is as inexperienced as I in that department."

"Oh dear, two virgins in bed is one virgin too many," advised Tamara.

"You have been with both men and women – do you have to be any different when it is the same sex?"

"Without the obvious biology lesson, John, it is not quite the same for two girls, but I understand your question. If there is a sexual attraction between you both, with you both being consenting adults, then sex will happen. Although a lot of people don't agree, it is quite acceptable. Why it never was is beyond me."

"So just 'go with the flow', then?"

"Yes, John, if it feels right," assured Tamara.

John Smith took the scroll of doomed names and entered the Realm of Death. As the office door closed behind him, he felt the reassuring comfort of the Realm that belonged to him alone.

He perused his list. The cords waiting to be severed in his realm began to appear in front of him...to his left, cords with dead ends; to his right cords with new beginnings...all waiting in line. The cords awaiting fulfilment...these were the mortal cords that appeared in the Realm of Death upon the conception of a child. He took hold of the first cord from the left, and with no emotion whatsoever, ended the life of a doctor on the Plane of Existence with a cut of his great sword. Sheathing the sword Whist holding the part of the cord that was still in his realm, he let the severed end wend its way back to the deceased medic. He then took the cord and added it to one on the right, placing them together. As soon as the two ends met, a flash of light fused the cords together, and the doctor was born again. John Smith carried on his task with gusto, wielding that great sword as only the Reaper can.

Back at the office, Tamara left for the evening, saying goodnight to the ever-efficient Mr. Braithwaite. Her first stop was the Pathology lab.

"Hello...it's quiet in here," observed Tamara.
"Isn't it wonderful? I was just about to put on some Mozart. I only have brief moments when culture can prevail in here," said Tom Harper.
"Tamara!" screamed Slabgirl, as she burst through the door.
"Alas, that particular avenue of pleasure eludes me once more. Now, how can I be of assistance?"
"It is a personal matter," said Tamara.
"Come to the office, we can use that while Mr. Jackson is away."
"Ah yes, poor Gavin, down with the flu," said Tamara.

"Yes, so it would seem. Excuse me one moment while I give the...for want of a better word...'student' something to amuse herself with while we chat."

Tamara laughed as she watched Sarah giving poor Tom a hard time. She wished she had a different personality to fall back on now and then.

Tom returned smiling. "That should keep the gruesome minx happy for a while. Now, how can I help?"

Tamara laughed again and said, "Gruesome minx?"

"Yes, she is – she loves this job."

"Is she good at her job?" asked Tamara.

"Oh, I wouldn't change her for the world! Working with Sarah is like being a bomb disposal operative. You have to treat the thing with kid gloves, or it will blow."

"You make her sound like a monster!"

"Oh, absolutely! she is the strangest person I have ever worked with at this place. She is untidy, her dress sense is deplorable, her intelligence debatable...although her devotion to her husband is second to none. She is a lovely person who couldn't hurt a fly...A strange contradiction! Now, enough about Gorezilla, you haven't come here to give me the counselling I so desperately need because of her, have you?"

Again Tamara laughed, especially about the *she couldn't hurt a fly* part. She was quite sure Atkinson would disagree with that one. At this point, Sarah made her usual backward bum door-opening manoeuvre. This time, the door handle caught the bottom of her miniskirt, pulling it upwards as she came through the doorway.

"If I have told you once, I've said a thousand times, put your white coat on!"

Sarah had now turned around with her skirt pulled up to her waist, revealing her white knickers with Moshi Monsters on the front.

"Sarah, it is a good job our mother can't see you now," said Tamara, with a slight grin on her face.

Sarah just giggled, trying to unhook herself from the door handle.

"Our mother?" echoed Tom.

"Yes, we are sisters...I thought you knew?"

"I had no idea!" said Tom, standing up and walking to Sarah. He took the tray of tea she was delivering, and then Sarah was able to free herself. "Your sister and I have things to discuss. There is blood on that table that I have been using...need I say more?"

Another flash of her underwear ensued, as she twisted at speed and ran to the waiting table. Tamara just shook her head and laughed.

"So, sister of swamp-thing, how do you like your tea?"

"Just like my men – strong with a hint of sweetness."

Tom smiled as he handed her the bone china cup and saucer used only for special guests. "So, here we are. I presume this has something to do with Mr. Smith?"

"Indeed, it has. Can we speak plainly, Mr. Harper?"

"Of course, we can, but please...call me Tom."

"Okay, Tom. You need to be careful in regards to John. He is not like any other man you may have met."

"In my line of business, the only men I've ever met are dead. It may be hard for you to understand, but believe me, when your work is Death you have very few friends. I was quite surprised when an accountant wanted to spend time with me."

"Hmm, quite – but that isn't what I mean. John Smith is a complicated man, and may seem odd at times, especially if someone angers him."

"Oh, believe me, I know...I've seen him in action."

"What do you mean?" said Tamara.

"The first time we were out, a group of lawless thugs came into the pub where we were, and one of them picked on John; within seconds, the whole lot of them were unconscious."

"I see – so you are not disturbed by that sort of thing?" queried Tamara.

"Contrary to popular beliefs, we do not all wear pink underwear and slap each other with our handbags. We are men, fuelled by testosterone – so no; it didn't disturb me at all."

"In that case, I can be a happy little secretary. There is one more thing I need you to be aware of – and that is, he has never done anything like this before, with a man or a woman."

"Then we had both better be careful, because neither have I."

"I can be at ease now. Oh yes, here's a couple of tickets to the opera for tomorrow night. I want you both to have fun, because he is going to be very busy after that for a while," offered Tamara.

"Thank you so very much! I tried to buy tickets for this opera, but it had been sold out for months!" enthused Tom.

"Yes, they are hard to acquire, that's where a good secretary comes into her own. I'm sure John and yourself will enjoy the evening, because apart from those being the best seats in the house they also offer you access to all areas, so if you want to chat backstage with the artists afterwards, you can," said Tamara, as she stood up and left the office. She kissed her sister on the cheek – the cheek that didn't have blood swiped across it, and left.

Under Crown Point Bridge, some people had gathered. These were low-life individuals drawn inexorably to that spot. They all just milled around, wondering what was going on. Some started fighting amongst themselves. When this happened, Crawshaw jumped down from his girder into the middle of the scrum. With one swipe of his arm, twelve bodies floated downstream. A circle opened up around Crawshaw, as he looked upon this ragbag army of misfits.

"Do as I say, and you will live. Displease me, and you will follow the shit that has just floated down the river," said Crawshaw.

Everybody moved aside as he strode through them, with more and more joining the ranks as he climbed back into the girders.

"I need sleep – see to it that I don't get disturbed."

The small army moved into position under the bridge, lining both sides, and the pathways along the bridges' top. As more people arrived, it wasn't long before the road spanning the river was blocked, alerting the police to the situation. There was no response from Park Road Police Station as it out of action, so police officers came from several other stations close at hand.

On arriving, the sight that greeted the police officers was unprecedented. Hundreds of people had totally blocked the road, and they were unresponsive to the requests of the police. More were arriving, some of them very well known to the law. The officer in charge quickly radioed in with the news that the situation was totally out of their control. Only an hour before, the road had been clear. He also instructed police HQ that there had been fatalities, as bodies could be seen floating in the river.

An air of pure hatred loomed over the place as the police tried to drive back the gathered crowd. Anguished faces stared out from the assembled mass, zombie-fashion. They began to sit down, and from the middle of the bridge where the crowd was at its fullest, the people began mumbling some incoherent words. The whole situation was becoming frightening. Suddenly the muttering stopped, and a deathly silence filled the air. The police drew back both ways from the bridge to wait for reinforcements from the army. A police helicopter flew overhead – the pilot and officer could not believe the sight underneath them. They also broke the news that the crowd stretched both West and East along the river on both sides. Crawshaw was protected to the max, as he slept in the Victorian girders of the bridge.

Away from the crowd at the river, in the North end of the town centre, two ladies were enjoying each other's company. Viktoria Malik was talking about clothes, clubs and bands. In fact, she was talking about anything rather than police work.

Linda Harper was mesmerised by the woman in front of her. She brought her hand up to the table and tentatively placed it over her companion's hand. Viktoria turned her hand around, and took hold. Both ladies smiled at each other, and in that tender moment, the tension of the first meeting vanished.

Viktoria lifted up her other hand, and Linda took hold of that, too.

"You are a stunning girl," murmured Viktoria.

"You are beautiful," answered Linda. "What now?" she continued.

"You mentioned earlier about there being more leopard skin on your person," quipped Viktoria, raising an eyebrow.

"I did, didn't I?" answered Linda. "Well, we should go...I don't think it would be appropriate to show you here," she continued.

Viktoria Malik paid the bill and took hold of Linda Harper's hand once more, and the two of them left the restaurant. As they arrived at Linda's apartment, the lower-ranked police officer asked, "Would you like a glass of wine?"

"Hmm, that would be lovely," accepted Viktoria as she looked around the small but very well-kept living room/kitchen.

Linda returned with a bottle of nondescript white wine and two long-stemmed glasses, handing one of them to Viktoria as they both sat down. After she had unscrewed the top off the bottle, she poured the wine very elegantly into Viktoria's glass. She then poured her own, and put the bottle down. An awkward silence filled the next few seconds, broken by Viktoria.

"So, your brother is a local pathologist; he never told me that."

"Yes, he never talks about his work. He learned his trade, so to speak, and qualified under Dr. Grayson. After Grayson retired, he then began working with a rather brilliant young doctor called..."

"Gavin Jackson?" interrupted Viktoria.

"Yes! He totally admires Dr. Jackson's skills and methods, and his understanding."

"I have never personally met him, but I do remember Chief Inspector Thompson took a while to adapt to the change after Dr. Grayson retired."

This small talk carried on for the next hour, until it dried up. To prevent another awkward silence, Linda said, "It's getting late…do you want to stay? It's totally up to you, I'm not…"

Viktoria placed her forefinger on Linda's lips and said, "As a police officer, you wouldn't want to encourage me to drink and drive, would you?"

Linda smiled and stood up, reaching out. She grasped Viktoria's hands, and helped her to her feet. As they walked out of the living room, Linda flicked the light switch to its 'off' position, and looked forward to the night ahead — a thought shared by the new person in her life.

The next day arrived, and Tamara was already up and dressed. Her choice of clothing that particular morning was most definitely casual. She was meeting Atkinson, to take part in her second favourite sport — clothes shopping.

Atkinson was already at the meeting place — a small café in the middle of town. Like always whilst he was in Administration, he used public transport to get around, and not teleportation. For times of pleasure, he encouraged his staff to use that mode of transportation as well. Tamara's taxi pulled up outside the arranged meeting place; she alighted and made her way inside.

As she approached Atkinson's table, her favourite beverage was waiting for her.

"Good morning, Tamara," said Atkinson. "A little late, my beautiful one?" he continued.

"Yes…there is a disturbance on one of the bridges across the river…it is causing all kinds of delays with traffic."

"Which bridge?"

"The old one by the Royal Armouries," said Tamara.

"I think we will go there; I want to deliver a message to someone."

"But I thought we were going shopping!" said Tamara, sporting a tremendous pout.

"This is business, Tamara. See you at the South end of the bridge."

As she finished her beverage, Tamara noticed a lovely lady watching her from a nearby table. On her way out, she placed her hand upon the woman's own, smiled, and gave her a business card, as she walked away, the young woman who was having a wonderful day looked over the card, quickly placed it in her bag and hoped their paths would cross again.

With that Atkinson and Tamara left the café, pulled their hoods over their heads, and disappeared, reappearing at the South entrance to the bridge. Upon their arrival, the entire crowd looked gaunt, and anger spewed from them. Atkinson looked at Tamara as he observed that any police presence had gone, and there were no helicopters taking photographs. He put that down to the crashed police helicopter's tail sticking out of the river.

As the crowd of what could only be described as zombies began to shuffle towards him, he lifted both arms up to shoulder level, his palms touching each other, then quickly separated his hands outwards.

The effect was reminiscent of the parting of the waves, as the entire crowd was ejected over both sides of the bridge, instantly clearing it. He jumped over the side and looked up at the girders, saying, "Don't use humans...as you can see, they offer no defence against me." Knowing Mother Nature wasn't ready yet, and neither was he, he turned and walked away.

Crawshaw stared from his vantage point and growled. The river was full of dead bodies, his entire army slain...carcasses were caught in the weir, in the locks of the canal, and floating downstream. As the police – bolstered by the army – finally arrived back, it was quickly realised that a mass suicide had taken place in some kind of cult event. The whole area was cordoned off. Ten minutes later, Atkinson and Tamara arrived at Wednesday's Wardrobe, to peruse new items to add to their own extensive ones.

Linda Harper's tranquil moment watching Viktoria Malik as she slept was taken away by her new lover's phone ringing. Viktoria opened her eyes, and took a moment to realise where she was, but instinctively answered the phone.

She glanced at Linda Harper, and then suddenly remembered everything as she answered the phone. She gazed at her beautiful new friend, and then leaned over to kiss her, saying, "I have to go Linda; when are you at work?"

"Today and tomorrow are my days off this week," she answered.

"Can we meet up tonight?"

"I would love that," nodded Linda, as she watched Viktoria dress. Once fully clothed, the Detective Superintendent leaned back down to kiss Police Officer Linda Harper on her lips, and then left the bedroom

Arriving at the bridge incident, Viktoria Malik quickly took charge and began to assess the situation. Talking with one of her junior officers, he relayed to her the facts of what had happened.

"You are telling me all these people just committed suicide? How come there are no survivors? Isn't that a little unusual for a suicide cult? Also, why do it in the glare of publicity? I think we'd better look into this a good deal further before we talk about mass suicide," said Detective Superintendent Malik.

"The bystanders are not much use at the moment."

"How so?" enquired Malik.

"It is as if they have all been briefed to say the same thing."

"Or they are all telling the truth..."

"Well ma'am, with respect, I don't think they are."

"Why?"

"Again, with respect, they are all saying they were drawn here against their will. Most of them who say they saw what happened said a man and a woman arrived at the bridge. The man held up his arms, then parted them, and as he did so the people started jumping from the middle of the bridge or were somehow thrown them over the side walls, landing in the river – one on top of the other. The couple then just disappeared. Also, most of these people are known to us...they are petty criminals and in my opinion, liars, ma'am."

"What about that downed helicopter over there?"

"Again ma'am, from our viewpoint, all we could see was it coming down. They must have had a weapon of some kind."

"Good grief, Detective Sergeant! We have hundreds of bodies floating in the river...a police helicopter crash, presumably killing its occupants...and people milling about, all saying the same outrageous thing! I need answers, and I need them fast! I want to know what's going on here! Has anyone checked the CCTV for the bridge? If not, why not? Please, make that your first job!"

"I will get someone straight on it, ma'am!"

"No! You do it! I want answers by lunchtime!" demanded Malik.

As she moved to the side of the bridge and looked over, she saw a man walking – away from the area, obviously a vagrant, by his appearance. When she glanced again at where he had been, he had vanished...it seemed into thin air. She said out loud, "I thought I saw someone I knew..."

As the 'vagrant' made his escape, he knew that the police had far more to deal with than a missing person and a Chief Inspector with a bad attitude. However, Crawshaw underestimated the tenacity of Chief Superintendent Viktoria Malik

JOHN PAUL BERNETT

Chapter Twelve

erusing the clothes at Wednesday's Wardrobe, Atkinson pulled out an item that looked out of place in the shop. It was a lime-green top made of a strange material, with a flashing sign on the front. Tamara was engrossed in the shoe department when Wednesday, who was looking more spectacular than ever, her mohawk adorned with feathers and jewels, walked over to Atkinson.

Her makeup was as dramatic as always; her drawn eyebrows were far exaggerating her natural brow line, and under them was an explosion of colour that greatly outstretched the edge of her eyes. Her jade-green lips matched the beautiful colour of her eyes. She wore a simple sheer crop top, which was displaying the outline of her breasts. A long black skirt, shredded about the hem so its appearance was that of being tattered, accompanied the daring top. The ensemble completed by a pair of six-inch platform Demonia patent leather boots. She saw the confusion on his face.

"Are you not a fan of Cyber-Goth, Sir?"

"I have never heard of it," said Atkinson.

"It isn't to everyone's taste," she said in her Southern-American accent.

"Indeed not! You have a wonderful accent, my dear, from where do you hail?"

"I do love how ya'll talk! I'm from North Carolina, the Deep South of America!" she said with a smile.

At this point, Tamara came over, and placed four pairs of shoes on the counter. "I love your outfit you are wearing today; it's gorgeous!"

"Thank you! Everything I wear, I sell in the shop."

"In that case, could I try that top you are wearing, please?"

"Of course, you can!" said Wednesday, showing Tamara the rail in question. Tamara disappeared into the dressing room and re-emerged wearing said item of clothing.

"How do I look?" she asked Atkinson.

"Wonderful...you must get that!"

Turning to Wednesday, she asked, "What do you think?"

"I think you look delicious," she said with a smile. "It brings out your femininity; you are a very beautiful woman."

"Thank you!" said Tamara, as she gave Wednesday a seductive smile.

The shopping continued over the next hour, and then they bid Wednesday goodbye and headed back to the office. Upon arriving, they found John Smith with a rather glum expression on his face.

"Whatever is the matter with you, John?" asked Tamara.

"I was all set to have lunch with Tom Harper, but he can't make it now, because his workload for the day has just massively increased."

"From what I have heard, you're going to be a bit busy yourself."

"Why?" said Smith.

"The first lot of Dark Realm Souls are ready for transference to the Realm of Nature."

"I didn't know we were ready for that."

"We aren't – it's a situation that cropped up just this morning. For the now, their cords will have to be tied off until we are ready."

"Well, as I have no date now – and I think I know who to thank for that, I may as well get to it!" said John as he stood and bid the two of them goodbye.

Upon entering the Realm of Death, the Reaper saw the cords hanging down. The despair contained in each separate one could be felt, even in that most desolate of realms. As he walked up to the first one, he saw someone holding onto it and looking straight at him.

"Now how have you managed to get into here?" asked a bewildered John Smith.

"I need to be the link between Atkinson, you and Nature – and I am here to tell you that you cannot begin until Nature is ready and Atkinson is fully in Administration," said Paladin.

"So, you are going to take part in this?"

"It would seem so..." he said in a soft voice.

"In that case, I will go back," said the Reaper. Paladin just smiled and nodded.

Back in the office, Tamara and Atkinson were sitting on the couch going through their acquisitions when John Smith opened the great door at the back.

"My word, that was fast, Smith!" observed Atkinson.

"I have just had an interesting conversation with Paladin," said Smith.

"Where? You have just returned from the Realm of Death."

"Indeed I have, but nevertheless, I spoke to him in there. He said we cannot transfer these souls until you are fully in your Administration."

"How can he be in there when you are in attendance?"

"Because...I have the ability to be anywhere and everywhere," said Paladin as he joined them. "But worry not, I will not enter a Realm without permission from you Atkinson, in the future," he continued.

Atkinson looked thoughtful and said, "This ability you have to be in the Realm of Death even though you do not hold Reaper status, and the fact that you can join the Reaper who is in Administration in that very Realm – where did you obtain such power?"

"Fear not, Atkinson. The permission or ability came from no one; it was all part of The Prophecy. I am the One sent to assist – or destroy, the Reaper of the New Age of humankind. With that in mind, I suppose you gave me the power."

"Assist or destroy?"

"Yes...this is not a regular occurrence. The Prophecy told of you taking over from your father, but went no further than that. Until all the Realms are brought together in harmony I am, shall we say, your Associate. I am an Associate for the good, but Executioner for the bad. There cannot be another like your father within our family."

"In that case, I look forward to your assistance – and thank you for your timely intervention with my Reaper."

"My pleasure," said Paladin, as he outstretched his hand in friendship.

Atkinson took his hand, and the two extremely powerful forces' friendship was sealed.

"How wonderful!" said Smith. "Let's take tea!"

"By the Gods, Smith, do you ever drink anything but tea?" said Atkinson.

"No..." he replied.

Tamara giggled and said, "Tea it is, then."

Far away from all of this, two young lovers were sunbathing on the white sandy beach that belonged to them alone. The sea was a turquoise millpond, very inviting and warm. Upon the smooth rocks that punched through the turquoise, mermaids were inviting them to join in their play. The sky was pale blue, and the sun hung low on the horizon.

Dixie took hold of Paul's hand, and the two ran towards the sea. As they entered the water, four mermaids dove in from the rocks. Dixie and Paul began to tread water as the four ocean angels popped their heads out of the sea, two of them taking Dixie's hands. The other two took hold of Paul's hands.

Although quite small in stature, these four beautiful mermaids were very strong, as one of them lifted Dixie out of the water and twirled her around. Droplets of water dripping from her naked body glowed like stars, as the low sunlight turned each one into a cascading, falling jewel. She was joined by Paul as he too was lifted from the water, and up to Dixie. Their bodies touched and they kissed as the mermaids swam in a circle, gently turning the couple they held aloft. Very slowly, all four mermaids began to submerge. Dixie and Paul felt the water rise past their knees, and then their waists...down, down they went until the sky was no more, and they were in the domain of the Sea-Folk.

Again, two mermaids took a hand each of Dixie's, and the same with Paul, and in unison their tails swished up and down. The two terrestrial beings felt an incredible surge of power as they were propelled forward. They were going deeper and deeper into the abyss.

The four sister mermaids made their way to a rendezvous point followed by all kinds of sea creatures...most of whom had never seen the human form and were very curious as to the sisters' new treasures. After a few short minutes, the mermaids, their guests and the cortege of all manner of sea creatures arrived at their destination.

To Johnson, it looked like they were entering a cave, but once inside he soon realised it was an entire city, part of which he had seen before on his quest for Atkinson's body parts. A surreal see-through wall now lay ahead of them, as the mermaids let go of their hands and began to tread water on their side of the wall.

Both Dixie and Paul gently pushed forward and passed through this bubble-like material into perfectly fresh air. Only now they realised for the five minutes it took to arrive there, they had been breathing sea water! They began to hear normally again, the sounds in their ears muffled by the sea no more. Dixie and Paul began to look around this undersea crystal kingdom.

The colours were of spectacular hues. Buildings made from crystals and humanoid creatures that seemed to be unaware of their presence were all around them. It wasn't too long before their presence was noticed, as a rather grey-looking being walked up to them. He turned sideways, and lifted his right arm in a welcoming 'come this way' fashion. Dixie and Paul lowered their heads slightly to acknowledge the being's actions, and walked past. The fact that they were naked didn't affect them, as all the beings around them were naked too. Anatomically, the grey-looking beings were similar to Dixie and Paul; the females had the same genitalia and breasts, and the males posessed the same genitalia as human men. The main difference was the pigmentation of their skin. Johnson put that down to the artificial light, but he was wrong.

An official-looking being came towards the terrestrial couple. He looked official, because from amongst a party of about fifty beings who were greeting them into their kingdom, he was the only one wearing clothes.

"Welcome my friends, it has been many millions of years since we have interacted with humans," he said.

"We are not exactly human, but thank you for your kind welcome," said Dixie.

"Our home is your home while you stay with us. We can fulfill your every need. Do you require sustenance?"

"No thank you, we have eaten already," said Johnson.

"Then I shall lead you to your room."

"Our room?" said Johnson.

"The One to restore the sea to its former state of grace is to be conceived in the sea," was the answer.

Paul looked at Dixie slightly puzzled, but followed the very polite official with her.

Above the ocean and on dry land, Atkinson and Paladin had returned to the Other Realm to discuss what was about to unfold.

Tamara was writing out that night's list, and John Smith was hoping Tom Harper could soon get through his backlog of work.

Tom Harper and Sarah were busy confirming that the cross-section of bodies delivered to the mortuary had all died of drowning, with no other sign of injuries apart from minor abrasions caused by their falls.

Detective Superintendent Viktoria Malik sat at her desk, trying to think of two things at once. The more she thought about it, the more she realised the two things were connected. The way Crawshaw dealt with the police at the station and the hold he seemed to have over her and the police officers was making her put the two things together.

"I want the search for Crawshaw increased. You might want to start by rounding up all the vagrants you can find...I saw one walk away from the bridge," she said to an assembled group of senior police officers.

"All our available officers are working on the bridge case," said one detective sergeant.

"Yes I know – I want that wrapped up for now. The coroner's office has said mass suicide. Get the river cleaned up and the helicopter removal arranged, we can return to that once we have Crawshaw in custody. Now let's make this happen fast, I have a bad feeling about the whole thing."

The meeting broke up and Viktoria Malik returned to her office. Picking up the phone, she rang the number Linda Harper had given her the night before.

"Hi Linda, it's Vik."

"Hello, I was just thinking about you," answered Linda.

"I was just wondering; do you fancy coming round to mine tonight?"

"I would love to."

"That's settled then! I will pick you up when I finish work. In the meantime, are you free in about an hour?"

"Yes, I'm just tidying my apartment."

"Can we have a working lunch? There are some things that I need to know about Crawshaw, and I don't want to spoil tonight with talk of work."

"That's fine with me."

"Great, I will pick you up in an hour."

"I will be ready," said Linda Harper as she put the phone down.

As things progressed on land, they got even better under the sea, for Dixie and Paul were now in their room. Although the walls were crystal-clear, there was perfect seclusion, because everyone had retreated to give the couple the privacy they deserved.

"What is going on?" asked Paul Johnson.

"I don't know, but this is a bedroom, and we are on holiday – and quite naked," answered Dixie with a smile.

"Yes! But all this glass, I wish it was frosted!"

The very instant the words left of his lips, the glass turned opaque. The couple looked at each other in amazement, as Dixie said, "We had better be careful what we say!" They both burst out in laughter.

Paul Johnson picked Dixie up, and walked over to the luxurious bed adorned with soft cushions and rose petals. The bed was huge and very inviting. As they lay down upon it, soft music could be heard, setting an ambiance for love. The mattress was water-filled; it was warm, and its movements lavished all kinds of sensual motions upon them, its gentle response exaggerating every move they made.

"So...what now, Mr. Johnson?"

"Now, Miss Dixie, we enjoy paradise, and all of its forbidden fruits."

"I don't think anything is forbidden here," replied Dixie.

"Life is good," said Johnson.

On terra firma, Viktoria Malik pulled up outside of Linda Harper's apartment and tooted her horn. Almost instantly, her lunch date appeared at the door and ran down the steps to the car. Leaning in, she gave Viktoria a kiss and said, "Hi!"

The two girls drove off to a nearby Italian restaurant. The restaurant was famous for its wonderful authentic food, and even more so for its singing owner. That day, the owner, who was past retirement age, was in good form and greeted the two ladies in Italian with her customary smile. Viktoria and Linda ordered a large mushroom pizza, which they shared, and two side salads. A bottle of white wine finished their order.

"This is the first time I've been here," remarked Linda.

"I love this place! While we wait for our food, let's get the business out of the way. For instance, would you have thought Crawshaw would turn against and kill his fellow officers?"

"I had him as a male chauvinistic pig, but not a murderer," said Linda.

"What was he like in day-to-day work?"

"He worked alone mostly; he had a bad attitude for sure, but to me, he just seemed the same confused woman-fearer that all male chauvinists are. Until I saw him drag Sergeant Simpson over the front desk, I thought of him as a mammie's boy. But that changed...it was like he had taken things a stage further...or was possessed or something."

"He has been in the police force for fifteen years, and his rise through the ranks was not a glowing one. I pulled his file today, and it did make for some very interesting reading. There were many complaints, but no real action taken. It seems he knows people in high places. But nothing within the file showed he had such a flaw in his personality."

The pizza and salad arrived, and the two girls tucked in. Talk of work was replaced with discussion of the previous night, and the night to come. Then the conversation changed to siblings, and in particular, Linda's brother.

"How old were you when you discovered you and your brother were gay?" asked Viktoria.

"I think we were both quite young; we were very close, as there are only eighteen months between us in age. We shared a lot of the same interests. I've never been a dominant female type, and I remained quite feminine throughout my early teens. Tom would play dress up with me. I think we would have been...12 or 13...when we realised we were not the same as other kids. That being said, we didn't know any other kids. What about you?"

"What about me? Now, there's a story! I was very late in coming out. I say 'coming out' because I am only out as far as a few personal friends are concerned – your brother Tom, for instance. My job kind of gets in the way if you know what I mean. I was silly enough to tell my parents – the result being I was homeless at 17 years of age – but not without money...my grandmother left me quite an inheritance in her will. So, I took myself off to University and got a little apartment, and kept my lesbian tendencies under wraps, just committing myself to work. I received the grades I went after and joined the police force, just like you, but I never told a soul. I tried the 'I will be a normal woman and get married', but it all came to a rather unfortunate end. I divorced several years back, and put love – and sex – on the back burner...that is, until I was bundled into the back of a police car whose driver took my breath away.

That day I took the biggest gamble of my working life and asked her for a date. I think that brings us up to speed," said Viktoria, looking straight at Linda.

Linda took hold of both of Viktoria Malik's hands as a tear welled up in her eyes. "That is the nicest thing anyone has ever said to me."

"It is how I feel; I know I am older than you, but I think we will make a great couple," said Viktoria.

"We already do; I will keep your sexuality a secret — no one will hear anything at work from me."

"I have a feeling that won't be a problem for much longer. I feel like screaming your name out to the world...I feel alive again!"

"Oh, look at the time!" said Linda.

"Good lord! We have gone on a bit, haven't we? I will take you back home."

"No need — I am taking Tom some lunch for a catch-up while I'm here," said Linda, holding a little plastic bag aloft.

"In that case, it's back to the grindstone for me," said Viktoria as she leaned over the table and kissed Linda.

"Text me your address and I will make my own way over to yours this evening," said Linda as Vik left.

The owner of the restaurant shouted, "Arrivederci, Bella signora!"

Linda just sat there smiling, with a wonderful, warm feeling all over. She picked up her bag and took out her purse, but the owner told her that her friend had paid. Linda just smiled and thanked the elderly lady, who shared the same parting gesture as the one she had when Viktoria left.

When Linda Harper arrived at the hospital, she made her way to the Pathology Department. She passed the laboratory and saw someone she knew through the window. On the other side of the pane of glass, Mike O'Sullivan, a lab tech, saw his friend and waved, saying, "Tom is in Gavin Jackson's office!"

She smiled and thanked him, and Mike returned back to his blood tests.

As she arrived in the mortuary, her gaze was taken towards the examination table, and to the young lady cleaning it, with no real attempt at modesty.

Linda smiled and said, "Hello, you must be Sarah!"

"I must be, because it says that on the badge on my white coat!"

"You don't appear to be wearing a white coat."

Sarah giggled and said, "You sound like my grumpy old boss!"

"That's because he is my grumpy old brother! I thought Mr. Jackson was your boss."

"He is as well; we are a tribe of three, and there are two chiefs and only one little Indian."

"That may be, but you are a very pretty little Indian."

Sarah smiled and was about to say something when Tom, having seen his sister arrive, came to her rescue.

"Run along now, you horrible little thing! Quickly Linda, come away, while you still have your sanity!"

Sarah stuck her tongue out at him and leaned back over the table to carry on her cleaning.

"Sarah! Where is your lab coat?"

"It has blood all over it!"

"Good grief! make yourself useful, and..."

"I know, make the tea..." she interrupted.

As Sarah left to go to the canteen, Linda asked, "Is she always like this?"

"It's because she needs feeding," replied Tom.

"Tom!"

"Yes, that's true! I haven't had any dinner, and it's nearly two o'clock!" came a voice from the adjacent room.

"Lunch — you haven't had any lunch, Sarah."

"Whatever you posh people call it, I haven't had any!"

"We can eat soon," said Tom, as he led his sister into Gavin Jackson's office.

"To what do I owe this wonderful pleasure? Nothing wrong, I hope?"

"Anything but! Tom, I have met someone!"

"Who is she, do tell?"

"Her name is Viktoria, and you already know her."

"Vik! Uh...sorry, Viktoria Malik?"

"The very same!"

"Wow! I thought she kept that sort of thing separate from her work, for obvious reasons."

"Yes she does, just like me. How long have you known her?"

"I know her from working here, obviously, but we struck up a friendship quite a long time ago. In fact, she is one of my few true friends," said Tom Harper.

"If we get close, that won't bother you, will it?"

"Your news doesn't bother me at all. I couldn't hope for a better partner for you! Hmm...with that in mind, I have some news for you."

"Do tell," said Linda.

"I have met someone too."

"Who is he? What does he do?"

"His name is John, and he is an accountant."

"Snore!"

"Actually, he is quite an exciting guy!"

"Is he? 'John the accountant' sounds a bit vague. What's his name?"

"His name is John Smith, and he works for..."

"Atkinson, Dewhirst & Smith?" interrupted Linda.

"How do you know that?"

"One of our old CID guys now works for them."

"Ah, yes, Paul Johnson! He is a friend of Gavin's!"

"This all sounds very nice, but I have to pamper myself now, so I am ravishing for Viktoria."

"You are such a whore!"

"I know, darling; do enjoy yourself adding and subtracting with the exciting Mr. Smith. Try not to get hot and bothered at the thought of his ledger"

"I will, thank you! Don't let the Detective Superintendent frisk you too vigorously...handcuffs leave marks, you know."

"Mine don't...they are fur-lined, sweetie."

"And you, a police officer! Get out of my office, tart!"

With that, Linda gave her brother a kiss, and turned just as Sarah was doing her door-opening routine. Linda watched the show, smiled and said, "Today is such a wonderful day!"

As she left the office, she gave Sarah a little tap on her bum. "See you later, Sarah," she said as she left.

Sarah looked at Tom and said, "So the sight of my bum does nothing for you, but your sister likes it?"

"Pretty much," answered Tom.

"Your entire family is strange! What about this tea?"

"Why don't we get our sandwiches out and have lunch?"

"Yeah, I'm starving!" enthused Sarah.

Back at the offices of Atkinson, Dewhirst & Smith, John Smith was looking thoughtful, and tapping his pen on his desk. He looked at Tamara as she was writing out that night's list and said, "When this is over, I wonder if Atkinson will stay on for a couple of days?"

"Why?" asked Tamara.

"I wouldn't mind going where Paul and Dixie are for a couple of days with...you know..."

"With Tom Harper?"

"Well, yes!"

"And how would you explain the two of you arriving at a South Pacific-type destination with nothing but elementals waiting on you hand and foot? And an island, I might add, that doesn't have an airport, a seaport, or any means of travelling to it?"

"Point taken."

"You could, however, take said boyfriend on a holiday by the usual means of travel."

"Do you think Atkinson will go for it?"

"Does she think Atkinson will go for what?" asked Atkinson.

"Where did you come from?" asked Tamara.

"I was just chatting with Paladin. It sounds as if I timed my entrance perfectly! So, Mr. Smith, ask your question, old boy."

"It will keep," said Smith.

"For heaven's sake! When all this is over, he wants to take his friend away for a couple of days," said Tamara.

"My dear fellow, if all this goes our way, you can have anything you desire! As for you Tamara, is your list finished?"

"Why yes, Sir, it is!"

"In that case, may I take you for a drink?"

"You most certainly can!"

"See you later, Smith," said Atkinson.

Tamara blew John Smith a kiss and said, "Bye, John!"

John Smith sat back in his chair and began to plan the first holiday he had had in, well, ever.

Gavin Jackson lay in his coma in the Other Realm, totally oblivious to what was going on, when his hand began to twitch. In a derelict building just outside the City Centre, Crawshaw released twelve souls from within. He had a mind-fix on Jackson, and dispatched his devotees psychically to the position where he lay. Once they had found where he was being held, they were to take over his body and bring him back. It wasn't easy getting into the Other Realm, but make it, they did. As soon as they arrived at the chamber, they saw Jackson at the far end. But in-between stood Dewhirst, in full armour.

On the Plane of Existence, Sarah drew a sharp intake of breath and dropped a tray of instruments on the floor. She instantly changed into warrior mode and disappeared. Tom Harper came out of the office to find the instruments and tray on the floor, and no Sarah.

Sarah materialized in the Other Realm, instantly tearing into the souls from the Dark Realm. Before any could get to her husband, she had freed them from their tormented existence.

"Hello, Sarah," said Dewhirst.

"No-one gets to my husband!"

"That is why I am here. I trust no one saw you disappear?"

Sarah just shook her head as she inspected the carnage that had just taken place.

"You are aware we need these souls?"

Sarah just looked at him and nodded.

Dewhirst noticed the power in which she had dispatched these once-powerful entities. Her muscle structure was quite pronounced as she stood there, her mighty broadsword in her hand.

"Crawshaw has found his whereabouts, so we must be on guard," said Sarah.

"Tomorrow it begins, as Atkinson starts his Administration properly," said Dewhirst.

"Tonight I stay with him – nothing will get through," said Sarah.

After what seemed a very long day, Detective Superintendent Malik left her desk to make her way home. On the way, she picked up a bunch of flowers, and the ingredients for the evening's meal. Her head was full of the approaching night with Linda Harper.

As she pulled into her driveway, she couldn't help but smile. Maybe it would halt further advancement, but she had decided that she was going to hide no more. Something was stirring deep within her, and she wanted to shout it out to the world. She wanted to walk down the main street of town, holding hands with Linda. Oh yes, now was the time. The closet had become a cold and lonely place – this was the 21st century, so no more pretence. She had a feeling of euphoria as she made her way up to the bathroom, casually throwing her workday clothes into the nearby washing basket. She stepped into the shower and washed away the day's blues. As she felt the bubbles caress her skin, she was glad she had a large shower cubicle, the kind that easily holds two people.

Her mind drifted to showering moments to come. She even dared for the first time to hope for love. Stepping out of the shower, she slipped into a dressing gown and wrapped a towel around her hair, as she made her way back downstairs to the kitchen.

Her kitchen was small, but expertly-designed around her needs. Everything was at hand, as she took the two ribeye steaks from the fridge. After seasoning them, she placed them on a grill pan. She then tossed a salad. The meat was cooking nicely, and the salad, with French dressing, was finished and placed back in the fridge. Viktoria poured herself a glass of wine, leaving the kitchen and placing a CD in her music player. The CD in question was Some Girls Wander By Mistake, and it just took the edge of the quietness away.

The doorbell rang, and she realised that she hadn't dressed yet. She opened the door, and standing there was a vision of beauty. Linda Harper had tied her hair up; her dark-shadowed eyes with black liner caught Viktoria's gaze. She was wearing a nose ring, and her lips were luscious and pale in colour. Her necklace was a dog collar, with studs adorning its length. Her black mesh top hid nothing of what lay underneath. The tightest of skinny-fit PVC trousers revealed a pair of legs a catwalk model would be proud of, and to finish the look, a pair of very high-heeled black stiletto shoes. Viktoria's mouth hung open as she gazed at her. Linda asked, "Am I too early?"

Viktoria stared at her and said, "I'm not dressed...uh, not ready..."

Linda placed her hand on Viktoria's chest and pushed her inside. "You look ready to me," she said, taking hold of the dressing gown and pulling it apart. The gown dropped to the floor, and Viktoria, apart from the towel on her head, stood naked in the hall with the front door still open. Linda placed her foot at the bottom of the door and slammed it closed. Viktoria threw her arms around Linda as she tingled with excitement.

In a lover's clench, the towel fell from her hair. Linda began to kiss her neck, and then her lips. The spontaneous situation Viktoria found herself in was the first time anything like this had ever happened to her. Her body was in a frenzy of excitement, and her mind was racing. The kiss seemed to last forever, and the situation was clearly as exciting to Linda, as the mesh top could not restrain the extensions of pleasure showing from beneath.

This love tussle found its way into the living room, where Linda placed Viktoria on the couch. After spending much of her adult life ordering people around, this was a new and invigorating feeling. The helplessness and adoration of this strong lady that was undressing in front of her were overwhelming. She was tingling with excitement – excitement that grew with each item of clothing her lover removed. After her outer clothing had been stripped, Linda Harper stood in front of Viktoria in a simple pair of white lace knickers. As she took a step closer, she offered her mate the priviledge of removing the piece of beautiful lingerie. Viktoria placed a forefingers and thumbs on Linda's underwear, and ever so gently pulled them down her legs, her gaze not moving from her lover's eyes. If she had dared to glimpse at the expertly-cultivated area of Linda's womanhood, she believed in that exact moment she would explode uncontrollably.

So there she was; this wasn't like the previous night, when two very nervous women had finally gone to bed without either removing their glance from the floor. This was pure, unadulterated lust – powerful lust that needed sustenance. And these two ladies were going to take it to the max. For Linda Harper, this was the first time in her life that she had taken control of a situation like this. Normally, it would have been the other way around, but the passion of the moment, as she saw Viktoria in her dressing gown, had taken control of her. The lovemaking was also different to the previous night, as the night before had been confined to slight touching, gentle caressing and fondling.

166

They found themselves on this night in the throes of wanton lust and desire. Many pent-up emotions were released that night – a night of change for both women – and the night was young. As for the dinner...well, the dinner could wait.

JOHN PAUL BERNETT

Chapter Thirteen

Far away from what was going on in the living room of Viktoria Malik, Paul and Dixie opened their eyes on the last day of their break in that wonderful paradise island. They were back on the beach, and Paul Johnson said, "I have just had the weirdest dream."

"No, you haven't," replied Dixie.

"What do you mean?"

"We were there together. We swam down with mermaids. We met the people of the sea, and made the most passionate love on the biggest waterbed I've ever seen," said Dixie.

"How did we get back here?"

Dixie pointed at the mermaids sitting on their rock.

"Whoa!" was Paul's simple reply. "What now?" he continued.

"A tingling down our spine and a sudden sharp movement, I suppose, and then we'll be back in the office."

"Well, let's get some clothes on; I don't want to be responsible for making Tamara's eyebrow dance."

Dixie laughed and said, "You should be honoured that the Listmaker finds you attractive, I know I would be."

"Do you mind? You are talking to a nearly-married man! And you, my girl. are a nearly-married woman!"

"I know, I'm just saying..."

"Yes, well...let's get dressed," he interrupted, slightly pink around the cheeks.

The couple dressed and had some lunch, then were whisked back to the office.

"For an accountancy firm, your mathematics are rubbish! I make that two days, not three!" said Johnson, as they arrived back.

John Smith laughed and said, "The game is afoot, old boy."

"What do you mean?" asked Dixie.

"Crawshaw has made his move on Atkinson; he tried to make contact with Gavin last night."

"I see," said Paul Johnson.

At this point, Atkinson joined Smith, Tamara, Dixie and Paul.

"Did you have a nice rest, and take care of that small amount of business, boys and girls?"

"The being grows within me as we speak, Sire."

"What grows within you?" asked Johnson.

"All in due course – we now have to begin. John, at eight tonight, I want you inside the Realm of Death. Tamara, I want him to have at least three nights' worth of lists. Dewhirst is on that as we speak. Sarah needs to be relieved, so Dixie, off you pop – that's a good girl."

Dixie disappeared, and Sarah appeared in her place, her sword still dripping with blood. She quickly changed back into normal mode.

"We are all here now," said Atkinson.

"What about Paladin?" asked Smith.

"He is liaising with Nature over the transference of the souls," informed Atkinson. "It is time for your investigation to begin, Paul. You might want to start with the Superintendent who is on the case."

"Do you know who it is?" asked Johnson.

"Malik, I believe."

"Oh, Vik...I know her quite well. If she is in a good mood, I will be able to work with her," said Johnson.

"Right, off you go then," said Atkinson.

Paul Johnson left the Reaper's office and made for his own.

"Ok, so here is the plan..."

Hanging on Atkinson's every word was Smith, Tamara and Sarah, as he laid out in fine detail the plan of action. After a few minutes, everyone in that room knew their role. Only Sarah brought a question to the fore.

"Are you sure Paul Johnson will survive this?"

"What – survive being killed, you mean? How many times have you killed me, Sarah?" asked Atkinson.

"I think this is a bit different," said Smith.

"There are risks, yes...a lot of things could go wrong. But at the end of the day, this is the only way we can get the souls that we need out of Crawshaw, so this is the way it will be."

With those words the meeting was over. They all knew the parts they each had to play, and most of them knew the risks.

A multitude of rats gathered around the old building whose only inhabitant was one Chief Inspector and the army of tortured souls within him. He was powerless, and barely alive. The awful Police Detective that he had been paled into insignificance as to what he had become. The rats milled around him as he prepared for battle with the offspring of the foe who had imprisoned the souls he held within him. He had the mind-link to get him into the most sacred of places – the Other Realm – a Realm in which he could undo Creation itself. As he knew the wretched body he possessed could not sustain him much longer, he needed an Immortal, like the female he used earlier. That was his first goal. The one he had the mind-link with was, for some strange reason, showing no resistance whatsoever.

Dewhirst had sent the three lists to Tamara, who in turn had written them down, cross-referenced them and passed them onto Smith. Smith and Atkinson looked at each other as the time drew close for Smith to enter the Realm of Death, knowing that he would be there for some time.

"You understand that once you go in there, my Administration will begin, and for the first time in existence there will be two Reapers at the same time?"

"I understand, and I will await your call," said Smith, as he entered the Realm of Death through the great door behind his desk.

As soon as the door closed behind Smith, Atkinson felt a jolt of power pass through his body, and a quickening of his senses. He looked at Tamara and said, "Oh yes, I am back!"

"No you're not – it is only for a few days, and you are a full day early," advised Tamara.

"My hand was played for me when Crawshaw made contact; I had to pull things forward. The fact is that we are ready...I just hope Nature is."

Within Mother Nature's Realm, a meeting was taking place between Paladin and herself. Again, it was held at the gathering place for the Centaurs. The most knowledgeable ones were in attendance.

"The Legion of the Dark Realm is concealed within the human being named Crawshaw. While this is the case, things are going to plan. Unfortunately, most plans don't run the course they are supposed to. We must assume this will be no different, so a backup must be in place from the start."

"Why doesn't Atkinson just kill Crawshaw?" was the murmured answer from many.

"Because Crawshaw's time isn't up! We don't want a situation where the all-powerful Reapers start killing at will!"

"But just one doesn't matter in the grand scheme of things, surely..." answered the Centaurs' leader.

"One, one hundred, one thousand, one million...where would you draw the line? No! The Reapers work within tight tolerances, and that is the end of it!"

"Mother, what is your plan?" asked Paladin.

One of the other Centaurs was about to speak; Paladin raised his hand very gently, and the Centaur's voice was silenced.

"I need a direct link between here and the Realm of Death, and Atkinson has provided it by initializing two Reapers. Atkinson will engage the Dark Souls on the Plane of Existence. Smith will accept them into the Realm of Death, but instead of cutting their cords and letting them go back, he will transfer them to me. Here is where you come into the plan, Paladin...There is no direct link between the Realm of Death and the Realm of Nature, the two must be kept apart in the same way that matter and anti-matter must be. Smith will send the souls via you – you are the common link between us," explained Nature.

"I see – will it be the portal in the woods?"

"Yes, it will – the very place from where they emerged. They will be purified through you, and then come from you not as a soul, per se, but as energy...the energy source that will be used to help rebuild the planet whilst you take your place as Atkinson's Apprentice, and help me heal the world. All we can do now is wait for Atkinson and his Warriors to do their part."

"You won't be able to use this energy straight away, so where will you store it?" asked Paladin.

"I will store it in the sap of trees, in the wings of birds; I will store it in magical places humankind has long since forgotten. Within my Realm, there are many vaults where power can be stored. It will be the Earth's bank account – and the first withdrawal, now that those weapons of mass destruction have been eradicated, will be for the ozone and its regeneration."

"Is everything in place for you to start receiving this energy?"

"Nature is ready for the transfer."

"Then I shall go to Atkinson and pass to him your message of hope," said Paladin, as he left the Realm of Nature and re-entered the Plane of Existence.

Once there, he called for Juliantrium. The whooshing sound of a large pair of flapping wings and the whinny of a unicorn resonated, as through the tree tops flew Juliantrium. She landed, and came to a stop beside her Master.

"Um...I think a winged unicorn may be a bit out of place here...perhaps something a little less conspicuous?" advised Paladin.

Juliantrium looked at Paladin and said, "How's this?" She turned into an E-Type Jaguar.

"It is beautiful, Juliantrium...but perhaps something a little easier on the planet? After all, we are here to try and save it."

Juliantrium instantly turned into a sit-up-and-beg bicycle. "What about this?"

"I don't think so – I need to fit in, especially with the young people."

This time, Juliantrium morphed into a skateboard with a pair of high-top canvas boots fixed to the deck. "Hop into them!"

With a look of reluctance, Paladin placed his feet into the boots, and as soon as he did, the skateboard propelled him forward, leaving his hair trailing behind and the wind in his face. Paladin's clothes changed as he stood on the board; he now wore a very baggy black t-shirt with the logo of the rock band 'A Day to Remember' across his chest, a pair of baggy black jeans, and a black baseball cap. A pair of glasses finished off the ensemble. He looked just like a thousand other kids around 18 years old, which was how he wanted to be.

Also on the Plane of Existence, Paul Johnson was in the car park of Police Headquarters, waiting for Detective Superintendent Viktoria Malik to leave the building. After about 40 minutes, she came out through the double doors.

"Hello, Viktoria," he said.

"Hello, Paul; you've chosen a bad time I'm afraid, I'm quite busy."

"This won't take long," answered Johnson.

"What won't?"

"I think we both know, Viktoria – we are both looking for the same man, and I can lead you straight to him."

"You have my undivided attention! I was going to get someone to take me where I'm going – that someone is now you. I was very disappointed when I heard you had left us; you had a glowing future in front of you."

Paul Johnson just smiled as he held the door open for one of his ex-bosses to get into the car. "Where to?" he asked.

"I am on my way to Park Road, your old stomping ground, Paul."

"Indeed, it was," Paul replied.

While getting in the car, Malik said, "Fire away."

"Your Chief Inspector Crawshaw has been a naughty boy."

"Oh yes? Why do you say that?"

"Well for one thing, he was the last person to see our secretary."

"Yes, but that doesn't mean anything."

"I don't have time for this Viktoria; do you need me to tell you what I know about this man, or not? For instance, do you want me to tell you why you are chasing him? That I know about the massacre at my old station, and the tramp you search for, as we speak? And why Crawshaw is at the middle of your bridge fiasco...do I need to go on, or can we drop the pretence?" said Johnson.

"How on earth could you possibly know all that?" gaped Viktoria Malik.

"As you say – I had quite a future in front of me. I am...was...a good cop."

"Okay, pull over there," said Viktoria, pointing at an available car parking space on the other side of the road.

The car pulled up outside a small café.

"Let us tell each other our secrets over a coffee," she continued.

They both exited the car and went inside the café. Passing the counter, Viktoria turned to Paul and said, "Strong and milky please." She then took a seat in the corner by the window.

Paul Johnson ordered the beverages and carried them to the table.

"Crawshaw seems to be part of some kind of suicide cult," said Viktoria, opening the conversation after she had sipped the bubbles off the top of her coffee.

Johnson pointed to the top of his lip, indicating that she had a bubble moustache. A simple lick with the tip of her tongue across her lip eradicated that particular problem.

"Suicide cult?" said Johnson.

"Yes – I saw the effect he had at the police station – I was there, and only just escaped...thanks to Sergeant Simpson bundling me into a police car and officer Harper getting me away from there."

"You could not have been saved by two better police officers."

"I know – I owe them my life. Anyhow, when I arrived at the bridge carnage, hundreds of people were dead in the water. As I looked over the bridge, I saw a vagrant walking away, and somehow, I knew the vagrant was Crawshaw. What I didn't know was why now? He only received this position at Park Road a short time back. He had one or two, let's say, disciplinary issues...that would make you think he would keep a low profile, not turn into this."

"His mind is going. Has he said anything to anyone about the company I now work for?" asked Johnson.

"Atkinson, Dewhirst & Smith?" said Malik.

"Dixie told us he had evidence that our company was murdering people, and this evidence placed our Mr. Atkinson at the scene of every unsolved murder that has taken place here over the last 50 years! According to him the reason our Mr. Atkinson had escaped conviction was because he was indeed the 'Grim Reaper'!"

"Good lord! He thinks he is chasing the Grim Reaper? This is ludicrous! We have to find this man! By the way, who is Dixie?"

"Come on Viktoria, sharpen up! She is the missing secretary; she said he has all this damning information in a file, locked away in a drawer."

Viktoria shook her head in disbelief and said, "That is our next move then...I shall check his files as soon as I get there. Imagine if any of this got out to the press!"

"May I come with you? This does involve me, as I am Head of Security at Atkinson's."

"You are a civilian, and you know quite well you can't," advised Viktoria.

"What if I could tell you his exact whereabouts, and where he will be tomorrow at precisely 10:00 p.m.?"

"How could you possibly know that?"

"How could I possibly know any of the other things we have discussed?"

"Oh, what the hell, come on then. Let's check this 'damning piece of evidence'."

They drank their coffees, exited the café, and got back into Johnson's car.

Upon arriving at Park Road Police Station, they found it was still cordoned off, with police guarding the building. A uniformed officer opened the gate, and Detective Superintendent Malik showed him her warrant card. Johnson parked in the car park, and they both exited and made their way inside.

The building was quite empty, apart from a couple of forensic officers taking the last of their samples. Johnson looked around the rebuilt police station, and could not believe the damage that one man caused as he followed Malik up to his old office. Once inside, she quickly went to the desk, and started opening the drawers.

"The bottom one will be locked," said Johnson.

"So is this top one – it has a padlock on it."

"May I see? I don't think that is locked, it's just stuck, as I recall," said Johnson, knowing that that lock didn't exist when he used to sit behind that particular piece of mundane office furniture.

He stood in between the desk and his companion, shielding the view of the lock from Viktoria. Upon placing his right hand around it, he gently squeezed, and the lock crumpled in his hand.

"See? The damn thing's broken, and it's finally given up the ghost."

Moving to one side, he let Malik open the drawer. There was a stack of pornographic magazines, a set of photographs of men and women in compromising positions, and underneath, a brown folder marked 'Atkinson, Dewhirst & Smith'. She took it out and opened it. The first thing to come out was a photograph of Dixie; she was naked and tied to a tree. Her head was hanging down, and you couldn't tell if she was dead or alive.

Then, she saw the 'damning evidence' that Crawshaw had in his possession which would elevate his police career even further – a set of drawings that looked like the doodlings of a six-year-old portraying the Grim Reaper swishing his scythe, cutting people in half, with the scribbled words, 'This is Atkinson!' written on the back of each drawing. There was a separate piece of paper which claimed, Atkinson was thousands of years old, and he changed every 25 years into either Dewhirst or Smith. The document was written in red crayon. Detective Superintendent Malik closed the file and said, "Chief Inspector Crawshaw is completely deranged. Take a look at this evidence!" She sat back in the chair, and offered Johnson the drawings.

"Where do we go from here?" said Johnson, desperately trying not to laugh.

"You said you knew where he would be tomorrow?"

"Yes I do; be ready with your officers tomorrow at 21:30 hours. As soon as he arrives at the place in question, I will ring you, and you can move in and arrest him."

"I don't understand why you can't tell me now..." said Malik.

"Because, I don't want anything to go wrong! Just be ready when I call. Now you can see that accountants are not as boring as you might have thought...just look at what they get up to in their spare time!" said Johnson with a smile on his face as he gave Viktoria Malik a wink.

As Johnson was leaving, his old boss smiled and said, "And what do I do with this folder of rubbish?"

"Keep it for evidence...at least we now know where Dixie is."

"We know she's tied to a tree...but that wooded area is vast! And by the looks of things, we are already too late," she continued.

"Late or not she has to be found. May I make a suggestion?" offered Johnson.

"Please do."

"I suggest removing a few officers from the bridge area, and having them perform an initial search of the wooded area. Then after Crawshaw is apprehended, put all of your available officers on it."

"Okay – I can afford four or five."

"Would you like a lift back?" asked Johnson.

"No thanks...I need to chat with the two guys downstairs. On a different subject, I assume you know Police Officer Linda Harper – do you know her well?"

"I know she's a good cop. A friend of mine works with her brother. Why?"

"Is she CID material?"

"My old Detective Sergeant used to think so...she was a friend of D.S. Donna Lambert."

"I wonder what made her think that way, It would be nice to know?"

"Donna told me on several occasions that she would have made a brilliant detective, but said there was something holding her back. However, she never told me what it was that indeed 'held her back'."

"Could it be her sexual orientation?"

Johnson looked puzzled for a moment and said, "I sincerely hope not! But I suppose she may have thought that she had no chance of promotion, so there was no point in applying."

"So, apart from her possible sexuality, do you think she would make a good detective?"

"Viktoria, you more than anyone should know that being a lesbian doesn't stop a person from getting where they want to go in life – I would have taken her on here as a detective any day of the week!"

Malik looked shocked and said, "What do you mean, I should know?"

"As you said yourself, I was a very good cop." Johnson smiled again, and left the office.

Closing the door behind him, he wondered if Tamara had a spare photograph of his beloved tied to the tree, when Dixie's voice rang out in his head…'Naughty boy'! He smiled again and made his way back to the car, and on to his office.

Outside the offices of Atkinson, Dewhirst & Smith, a young man did a kick-flip with his skateboard, and then placing it under his arm, he entered the building.

"Good day, Mr. Paladin! I shall announce your arrival," said Mr. Braithwaite.

"Just call me Pal, dude," said Paladin, getting into the spirit of his new look.

When he entered Atkinson's office, the head of the company said, "What are you wearing?"

"This was Juliantrium's idea," said Paladin.

"Do I take it that Juliantrium is under your arm at the moment?"

"I am indeed!" said a sweet voice emanating from the board.

Atkinson smiled and said, "You don't look as regal as you sound, my dear."

"We are like…disguised, dude!" said Paladin.

"You're disguised as the clichéd road-surfer," observed Atkinson.

Paladin just smiled and said, "It will keep me invisible for a while."

"Do I take it from this disguise that Nature and yourself are ready to begin?"

"We are indeed."

"Excellent! I will gather my troops," said Atkinson, his ancient adrenalin beginning to kick in.

The building that Crawshaw inhabited now housed the real army he needed. This army of rats could move without detection, and be in place in minutes within its subterranean world. Thousands of rats lay before him, and thousands of damned souls within him. The Beast knew his true power was while he was Legion. He also realised, however, that being Legion offered the quickest solution for Atkinson to dispatch him. He sat looking at his followers, pondering the decision. But patience was not his virtue, and for now, Legion would continue.

Crawshaw now transfixed his power of thought upon the one they called 'Sentinel'. Having sacrificed some of his minions to find the Sentinel's rough whereabouts, he now had an exact position, and that meant that he could get deep into the legendary being's mind. He lifted his hand and pointed forward. From the dark, damp writhing abundance of rats, a mischief of around fifty of them came forward. Again, Crawshaw lifted his hand and pointed. The screech of many tortured souls echoed across the room, as each of the fifty rats accepted its new consciousness. Each one then stood up upon its hind legs and awaited orders. Crawshaw telepathically passed the rats their instructions as he guided them through his thoughts to the very room where Gavin Jackson lay.

Dewhirst, this time accompanied by Dixie, stood guard over the Sentinel. The rats, now altered to quadruple their original size, materialised in front of them, but again were still not powerful enough to cause any damage upon the Sentinel's guards. Crawshaw was losing souls and not inflicting damage at all. The souls, dispatched into the Other Realm, went straight to Smith, who was waiting in the Realm of Death. Fifty souls were tied off to wait for transference, and fifty rats returned to the wild. That was the specification of Mother Nature at the outset of her original meeting with Atkinson. Atkinson and Sarah joined Dixie and Dewhirst.

"What was that?" mused Atkinson.

"A mere bit of mischief...nothing more," said Dewhirst.

"So he's going to use rats, is he?"

"It makes sense – they are readily available and easy to dominate," answered Dewhirst.

"As a pack of wild rats is not loyal, that could be to our advantage. The only thing is, it is clear he intends to separate the souls individually," observed Atkinson.

"They will be easy to find – the ones that attacked us were four feet tall!" said Dixie.

"Unfortunately, on the Plane of Existence, they will be normal-sized rats, so will be quite difficult to find," said Dewhirst.

"Is this the right way, Atkinson?" asked Sarah.

"What do you mean?"

"Gavin is lying here in a coma, because Crawshaw might use him to get to us. It would appear that it doesn't matter, as he is sending mercenaries to kill him! If you asked me, he doesn't want to use Gavin to get to you...he wants him out of the way so he cannot protect you! Bring him out of his coma...that way, he has a fighting chance against Crawshaw's minions, and he can help you!"

"It also frees Dixie and me for the upcoming battle," said Dewhirst.

"So be it," agreed Atkinson.

Atkinson walked over to the table where Gavin Jackson lay, and put his hand on the Sentinel's brow. Jackson instantly changed into warrior mode and sat up, much to Sarah's delight.

"Has there been enough time?" asked Atkinson.

"Yes...as soon as I detected Crawshaw's mind-trace I locked onto it. I now know the very building where he hides," said the Sentinel.

"Good... the plan worked," said Atkinson.

"The plan?" said Sarah.

"Yes – Crawshaw needed information. I knew he would go for one of you because of what he would have learned from joining with Dixie. I also knew that because of the human that the Beast had possessed, it would not be a female he went after. I needed it to be the strongest of my Warriors, but Sarah, you are female, so next in line was Gavin. The coma made it easier for Crawshaw to connect to him, and that was precisely the route he took. Welcome back, Gavin," said Atkinson, placing his arm around Gavin Jackson's shoulders. "We know where he will be, and we know what his army is. The Reaper, Mother Nature and Paladin are ready. We are ready, and at 22:00 hours on the morrow, we will attack this unworldly adversary, and put an end to the Dark Realm forever.

JOHN PAUL BERNETT

Chapter Fourteen

he Day of Judgment dawned on the Plane of Existence. Gavin and Sarah Jackson woke early from their slumber, with no trepidation for the oncoming fight. Dixie and Paul Johnson also stirred as the sun burst through the open curtains of their bedroom window, both of them knowing what lay ahead for them on that day.

Atkinson lay in bed as he observed Tamara through the open bedroom door as she showered. He had watched this beautiful woman bathe, dress and undress over countless centuries, and had never grown tired of the wonderful show. She walked into the bedroom, water dripping from her hair.

"Are you enjoying the show, Mr. Atkinson?" she said impishly.

"Indeed, I am – I am waiting for the second act!" he replied.

"The second act will follow later...we have business to attend to," she answered, as she wrapped a towel around her naked body.

"I'm beginning to hate this Crawshaw character," said Atkinson.

"Good! That will help you think like him!"

"I don't have to think like him – his thoughts are now passing to me through Gavin."

"You mean the mind-link is still open?"

"Yes – I have been monitoring Crawshaw all night."

"How long will this mind-fix stay open?"

"As long as it goes undetected. If Crawshaw realises what is happening, he will send all manner of confusing information, and we will lose our fix on his position."

"Let's hope he doesn't find out, in that case."

"That's like hoping he will keep all the souls within him; it would be nice, but very unlikely. As soon as he realises that Gavin is out of the coma, he will cut the link," said Atkinson, as he got out of bed and walked to the shower.

Gavin and Sarah were now up, both of them in their luxury penthouse double shower. As Gavin gently washed her back, he noticed her tattoo at the top of her arm, and the thin gold line passing through it. He remembered the first time it had glowed, heralding Dewhirst's visit, and how his badly-distressed leg became as new. He kissed the back of her neck, and realised what a lucky man he was. He'd married the funniest, strongest woman he knew. She could change from the strange little Slabgirl to the magnificent and all-powerful Earth Warrior – who feared nothing in any realm, from the Plane of Existence to the Dark Realm. She was beautiful and quirky; she had a simplicity about herself, yet was so complicated. If ever there was a contradiction in terms, it was his precious wife and comrade-in-arms – both of whom were his, and his alone. This knowledge was where the Sentinel's strength came from, for there is no power greater than love, and both of these people poured oceans of this wondrous power over each other.

Dixie, as ever, was up and dressed first. Paul Johnson was lagging behind as he came back from the shower, frantically drying his hair with a towel. Dixie laughed and said, "We do have elementals that will do that for you...it saves an awful lot of time you know."

"I'm quite capable of drying my hair, thank you very much. How come you use the elementals for, more or less, everything?" asked Paul Johnson.

"You would understand better if you knew what I used to do before I met you," answered Dixie.

"Why? What did you do? I've always wanted to ask you that."

"I was, and I suppose still am, an elemental. My tasks were looking after higher beings. I was never allowed to see them, nor have the opportunity to be a personal groomer...although, like all of my kind, I used to dream of being a personal elemental to the Listmaker. Her beauty was, and is, legendary. We all used to muse upon what she would look like, and what it would be like to serve her. Of course, the odds against reaching that dizzy high were the same, let's say, as winning the lottery every week for a year. My job was cleaning and washing, and at all times, I had to be kept out of sight. If seen by one of the Immortals, it meant instant dispatch."

"Why do you never use the word Death?" asked Johnson.

"Only the Reaper and powerful Immortals are allowed to use that word."

"Why?"

"Because it is a sacred word, and to use it is to accept your own," answered Dixie.

"I can see why you are enjoying life now," said Johnson.

"My life is unbelievable! I have you, and all this power within me, and nothing ties me down anymore!"

"Speaking of tying down, or should I say up..."

"Mister Johnson! I don't think we should be pondering such things today! We have to keep our minds clear for the task ahead!"

Paul Johnson had a little giggle and said, "I didn't mean now – What I was going to say was, when this is all over, I will have to tie you to a tree naked."

"Won't you be cold?" She asked, a cheeky smile adorning her face.

"Very funny," said Johnson. "But I will have to tie you to a tree in the woods," he continued.

"Do go on...what then?"

"Well...I will leave you there to be found by the police."

"I was enjoying it up to that point!" said Dixie.

In the Realm of Death, John Smith was enduring the longest spell any Reaper had dealt with within its solitude. He had spent time in the Realm of Death whilst guarding Atkinson's apparition, but this was different. While carrying on with the day-to-day cycle of Reaping and Sowing, he was also holding onto the souls removed from Crawshaw's grasp. These were the souls of murderers and unrepentant criminals destined for the defunct Dark Realm that were soon to be dispatched to Nature. The solitude had no effect on Smith as a Reaper, because he had lived so long on the Plane of Existence within abject solitude as Atkinson's Surrogate. In fact, he found the Realm of Death rather comforting, in a strange way. He felt a sense of purpose as he took a soul from an old, worn-out body and gave it new energy in the birth of a newborn child.

Yes, John Smith was enjoying his long spell of reaping, because he had time to think in its deep solitude, and the thoughts in his head were of a certain young man working in the Pathology Department at the hospital. He also wondered what Tom Harper would think if he ever found out that his new love was indeed the Grim Reaper. He pondered upon the thought of what Tamara would think of him using his time within the Realm of Death to think about Tom.

Tom Harper was in a much better mood that morning, because the pressure of running the department alone during a very busy time was at an end. He was so pleased to see Gavin Jackson and his macabre wife walk into the Pathology lab.

"Am I glad to see you, Gavin!" exclaimed Tom.

"I'm glad to be back, Tom! Sarah has told me how busy you have been."

"We have! Thankfully, we didn't have to check all the unfortunate people from the bridge suicide."

"Yes – that would have made for an awful lot of work. Were the deaths drownings, or were there variations?" asked Gavin.

"The odd bruise or two from the fall off the bridge, but apart from that, every one that fell over the bridge died by drowning," said Tom.

"Apart from the ones who got out of the water..." remarked Gavin Jackson, as he tried to hide the fact that he knew everything that had happened on the bridge, even though he had been in a coma at the time.

"That's just it – no one got out of the water, they must have just drowned where they fell. That was the reason for the 'death by suicide' statement that came from the police – because many of them could be seen still alive in the water, but they made no attempt to get out. It was almost as if something was guiding them to that end," said Tom.

"Okay...well, I'll leave you with Sarah so that I can catch up on my paperwork," said Gavin as he walked away to his office.

"And what, pray tell, are those things on your legs, madam?" said Tom as he stared in disbelief at Sarah.

"My trousers," answered Sarah.

"All I can see is your legs...trousers are not supposed to be ripped all the way up the front," said Tom.

Sarah swished around, and Tom nearly fainted.

"They are the same at the back...I can see your bum cheeks!"

"I have a nice little bum. Gavin says that all the time," said Sarah smiling.

"That is as may be, but do you think this is the place to have it on display?" asked Tom.

"It won't be on display when I have my white coat on, will it?" she said, sticking her tongue out at him.

"You drive me to despair! Just make sure it's fully buttoned up, lady!"

Sarah disappeared into the locker room, and returned wearing her fully-buttoned white coat, the largest pair of thick rubber gloves he'd ever seen, a surgical face mask and a pair of goggles.

"How do I look now?" she said.

"Perfect! Just stay like that, it is a definite improvement. By the way, what time is it?"

"I know, it's tea-making time!"

"Off you trot then, you little minx, and put yourself to good use."

Just as that particular conversation was taking place, Detective Superintendent Viktoria Malik came into the room.

"Hello, Vik...I mean, hello, Detective Superintendent Malik. How can I be of service?" asked Tom.

Viktoria showed a small grin as she looked at a very posh-sounding Tom Harper, and the bane of his working life, who looked as if she had just come from the set of an old Hammer Horror film.

"Do excuse whoever-she-is, she was just leaving," said Tom, pushing Sarah towards the canteen.

"I'm going to make some tea!" said Sarah.

"Then be gone with you!" said Tom.

Sarah turned and walked out, humming the death march. Tom just shook his head and rolled his eyes.

"Never a dull moment, eh?" said Viktoria, as she gave him a wink.

"So – is this business or pleasure?" asked Tom.

"Both...but business first. Is Gavin Jackson back yet?"

"Yes, he is – would you like to see him? He is up to speed on everything that has happened on the bridge."

"Yes I would, please."

"And the pleasure?" queried Tom.

"Would you and your little accountant fancy a night in the Show Bar with your gorgeous sister and me?"

"My 'little accountant', as you call him, has not been answering his phone – and his secretary told me he is out of town for a day or two on business, so I can't answer for him as yet, but I'm certainly up for it! As soon as he is back in touch, I will give you a ring," promised Tom.

"It's a date, then!" replied Viktoria.

Tom showed her to Gavin's office. After the pleasantries had been exchanged, Detective Superintendent Malik said, "Now that everything is cleared up and all your tests have been done, can you throw any light onto why, after jumping over the low bridge into the water, none of them changed their minds and got out? In my experience with suicide, many people change their mind – and the law of averages says that some of that large crowd would have done so."

"I don't think the law of averages comes into this. You speak of experience...may I ask, are you basing this experience on singular suicides?" asked Jackson.

"Well, yes...thankfully, we are not overrun by mass suicides in this town."

"Just as I thought...mass suicide is totally different to a person who just can't take anymore, and decides to end it all. These are cult-followers, people who are under the influence of a very strong personality."

"You seem quite knowledgeable on this subject."

"It is a subject I studied quite intensely. Can I offer you a drink, Superintendent?"

"No, thank you. So are you saying one person could be behind all of this?"

"Almost certainly."

"The more I am looking into this, the more one person's name keeps cropping up in my head. But it can't be...he is a..."

"Chief Inspector in the Police Force?" interrupted Gavin.

"Whatever makes you say that?"

"I am a friend of both the lady who is missing, and her partner Paul Johnson."

"What has he been saying about it?"

"Oh...he is still too much of a good policeman to cast wayward aspersions about anyone. The thing is, I was in the man's office when he saw Crawshaw man-handle his fiancée into the woods – after he had coerced her into many meetings – as he tried to infiltrate the actions of Atkinson, Dewhirst & Smith."

"We have to catch this guy," said Malik, as she stood up and bid her farewells.

Sarah came into the office with her husband's tea, and Gavin said, "I think we will soon be rid of this troublesome police officer."

In the cold, damp mill on the South side of the river, a voice rang out. "Where is the son of my jailer?" growled Crawshaw.

The rats just twitched their noses, with no real concern for their Master's question. He reached into the sleeping mind of Gavin Jackson with the same question, but to his horror, found the Sentinel wide awake. The question bounced back at him, with the answer, 'You will know soon enough!'

Immediately, Crawshaw cancelled the mind-link and stood up, displacing several rats from the floor with a kick of his boot.

The action that followed was two-fold: he had placed a certain amount of trepidation into Crawshaw, as he knew his position might be compromised. It also totally freed the Sentinel from any further interference from Crawshaw.

Crawshaw pointed at one of the nearby rats, releasing a captive soul from within. The rat instantly became humanoid. The creature walked up to Crawshaw, its neck still broken from the hangman's noose.

"I have the blood of a rat running through my veins."

"Better free with rat's blood, than being caged in that old realm...now get out of my face before I put you back there!" screamed Crawshaw, as he punched his soldier square in the face, sending him sprawling into the rats.

He began pointing at other rats, gifting them with murderous souls – all bent on revenge and destruction, but with no voice.

The old mill was filling up with murderers, rapists, and the dregs of ancient humans long since dispatched to the Dark Realm.

Crawshaw looked upon his army and declared that very soon, the Plane of Existence would be theirs for the taking. In unison, they each raised their arms in the air. With their clothes withered and torn, most of them with broken necks or horrendous burns from the electric chair, and none of them able to talk, all they could muster were moans of pain. They looked like the beginnings of a Zombie Apocalypse. Crawshaw surveyed his Army of the Dead, and was ready to face his adversary.

In the Other Realm, Atkinson called upon Sarah, Gavin and Dixie, all of whom appeared in front of him in battle dress, swords in hand.

"Now that Crawshaw has released Gavin from his mind, he will be aware that we know his whereabouts, which will mean the souls will no longer be within him. This will prove both troublesome and advantageous," instructed Atkinson.

"In what way, advantageous?" said Gavin.

"Now that he has separated, his strength is diminished in this realm. He is only so bold because of the strength he felt whilst he was intact with the other souls. The police can deal with him when he shoots...well, let's not worry too much about Crawshaw."

Sarah and Dixie both looked at Atkinson.

"Who will be shot?" asked Sarah.

"As I said, let's not worry about that, as it has no effect on what we are doing."

Sarah took out a small stone, and began sharpening her sword saying, "Be careful who you sacrifice, Atkinson."

Gavin and Atkinson both looked at the warrior with the cold steel in her eyes. She bore no resemblance to Slabgirl as she deftly sharpened her weapon of choice.

Dixie, who could not challenge anything Atkinson said, looked on, but she had the same fear of losing someone that Sarah felt.

Atkinson calmed the situation down by saying, "Can we sort this out without human emotions, please? We all have a job to do."

Dixie hung her head. Sarah just kept sharpening her sword.

"At exactly 22:00 hours, we attack the mill. Now, I must brief Johnson on his role in this battle."

With that, Atkinson left the Warriors with Dewhirst.

Paul Johnson was sitting at his desk watching the seconds pass, when Atkinson materialised in the chair in front of the ex-Chief Police Inspector.

"If I had been drinking tea, it would be all over you now!" said Johnson, with his pulse racing.

"You must get used to my untimely entrances," answered Atkinson.

"Can't you materialise at the other side of the door and announce yourself? It would certainly help my blood pressure."

"Your blood pressure is fine. You have arranged for a police presence at the old mill tonight?"

"I have; Detective Superintendent Malik will be there with a large police presence."

"Does the Superintendent know the whereabouts, and the time?"

"I have told her I will give her both at 21:30 hours."

"Good man! I want you and the police there at 22:00 – not a second later or earlier – Is that understood?"

"Clear as day," said Johnson.

"In that case, I will leave this in your capable hands. Just so you don't jump, I am leaving now," said Atkinson as he disappeared.

He reappeared in front of Tamara's desk. The Listmaker was buffing her already beautifully-manicured nails.

"Well, my day just improved!" quipped Tamara.

"The sight of you always brightens my day," smiled Atkinson.

"Judging by your armour, you haven't come here to rid me of my clothing, and do all manner of unmentionable things to me across my desk..." said Tamara.

"Alas, Tamara...no. I need a link to Smith."

"As you know, he is in the Realm of Death," said Tamara.

"And that is precisely why I need you," Atkinson advised.

"You want to talk to him through me?"

"Yes."

"Well, you're the boss...but I must say, this is most uncomfortable. I had to do it once with your father and Dewhirst."

"Why is everybody whiny today?" said Atkinson.

Tamara just raised an eyebrow and said, "Come and get me, tiger!"

Atkinson smiled and said, "You are such a trollop!"

"You'd better believe it!" she answered.

Atkinson sat behind her, and placed his hands at the sides of her head, and then concentrated on Smith.

I'm a little busy right now, Tamara, is what came through.

It's Atkinson – we need to talk.

Fire away!

Not like this, come to the door.

Seconds later, the great door at the back of the office opened with its familiar creak, and Smith walked in.

"What's going on?" enquired the Reaper

"Everything is in place...but, it isn't going to be as straightforward anymore."

"Why?"

"Crawshaw has split from the souls."

"I see, so what do we do now?"

"Instead of me sending them to you in one lot, it will be four of us sending them in smaller lots. Are you okay with that?"

"I don't mind how they come to me, I just need to know what time they will start arriving. Are they in human bodies?"

"They will start arriving at 22:00 hours GMT – but, they have taken the bodies of rats."

"I can't reap rats," said Smith.

"Normally that is the case, but this is different. It is just the soul that holds our interest. As soon as you have the individual soul, you will store it with the ones you already have by tying the cord, and not severing it. Once you have the soul, think 'Dewhirst'...and he will pass the rat's life force on to the correct Reaper."

"That all sounds fair enough; I will go back now and prepare."

"Good man," said Atkinson.

"Before you go, John, I have a message from Tom Harper. He wants to know if you are available to go out to the Show Bar with him, his sister and her partner," said Tamara.

"That sounds brilliant, after spending all this time in the Realm of Death! Answer yes for me, please!"

With that, he turned to the great door and returned to his work.

"So – we are about to go into battle, and you are arranging dates for the Reaper?"

"Life goes on...we can't let a little apocalyptic threat get in the way of true love, now, can we?"

Atkinson smiled at Tamara and blew her a kiss, saying, "It begins at 22:00 hours. Be ready, just in case."

"I am always ready," was Tamara's answer.

Atkinson disappeared and rejoined his Warriors.

Paul Johnson picked up his phone and rang Viktoria Malik. When she answered, he said, "I have the details you need for tonight's raid."

"Where and when, Paul?"

"The old disused mill just South of Leeds Lock at precisely 22:00 hours – not a second before, or a second after," said Johnson.

"That is not much in the way of tolerance," said Malik.

"That's as may be – but it is the tolerance you will have to work to," said Johnson.

"Okay, 22:00 hours it is."

"I will meet you at the main doorway," said Johnson.

"I think it would be better if you left it to the police," answered the Detective Superintendent.

"I can't leave anything to chance; things must be done exactly, and I know exactly what you guys have to do. You want to get this guy, don't you?"

"Okay, I suppose this is a somewhat unusual case. I will meet you at the entrance to the mill." With that, she bid him goodbye and began organising her team of officers who would carry out that night's raid. Paul Johnson put the phone down and left his office. He knocked on John Smith's door and walked in.

"Hello, Paul," said Tamara.

"Hi, Tamara."

"Yes, she is," said Tamara.

"What?" said Johnson.

"You were just about to ask me if Dixie is capable of what she is about to do."

"Yes, I was..."

"She, along with Sarah and Gavin, is a powerful force...and don't forget who will be fighting alongside them."

"Yes, I know all this...and I understand that a Reaper, a Scribe and a Listmaker must stay in situ, but..."

"Why is it me, and not Dixie?" interrupted Tamara.

"Well...yes."

"This is Dixie's first Administration with the Reaper. Her experience is very limited; she has never worked with a different type of Reaper, and doesn't have a full understanding of the job. I, on the other hand, do. It is that simple, Paul."

"But Atkinson is far more experienced than John Smith..."

"Yes, he is...and we are going over the same stuff as we did before. It's down to this, Paul – only four beings have a slim chance of killing Atkinson. One is his partner Dewhirst. Another is Mother Nature – and as long as he is doing her a favour by bending the rules to send the reaped souls to her, I think he is quite safe to have a little fun."

"Fun? Is that what you call it?"

"To Atkinson, rendering the Dark Realm asunder will be him laying the last thing that binds him to his father to rest. He can then get on with a much greater challenge."

"You said four beings."

"Yes I did, but I don't see Gavin or Sarah turning on him, do you?

"I see...so can you guarantee that Dixie will be safe?"

"There are no guarantees in this line of work, Paul...you might not survive this day yourself."

"I thought we were all Immortal."

"Yes Paul, we are...but only in the fact that we do not have a mortal cord, and a life number ticking downwards. If struck by the right weapon, we will fall."

"But Atkinson will bring you back to life, like he did before..."

"That would depend upon the weapons they have perfected in that miserable realm. Weapons made from hate are never good weapons, Paul."

Paul Johnson bid Tamara good day and left the office.

In the old mill just South of Leeds Lock, Crawshaw rallied his troops. The tormented souls using the life force of rats in human form all hung upon his every word.

"We will first kill all the Creator's soldiers, then we will kill Atkinson – the son of the Creator. When that small task is complete, we will ravage the Earth and find the creature known as Paladin. He will now be beyond turning to our way of thinking, so he will be put to the sword as well. Are you all with me?!" he screamed out.

Moans of agreement came from the mischief of humanoid rats.

As night began to fall, Paladin and Juliantrium drove to their position in the woods. Mother Nature had prepared a holding cell in the far corner of her domain, ready to receive the souls from Paladin.

John Smith had finished his shift of cutting the normal cords he had to deal with, and was awaiting the first of the Dark Souls to pass through his Realm of Death.

Johnson placed a loaded revolver in his shoulder holster, and made his way to the rendezvous point.

Tamara was waiting to pass telepathically from Smith the life force of the rats to their rightful Reaper System via Dewhirst.

Chief Superintendent Viktoria Malik and her police team were parked 300 yards up the road from the mill, ready to activate at 22:00 hours.

Atkinson, Sarah, Gavin and Dixie all drew their swords as the hour approached, then disappeared from within their Realm.

The Town Hall clock rang out ten resonating bells as Atkinson's Warriors reappeared in the mill. Mother Nature and John Smith opened a channel to Paladin, and Viktoria Malik and Paul Johnson, with the help of the police, charged at the door.

"Atkinson!" screamed Crawshaw, as he took his revolver from its holster and fired off three rounds straight at him.

Atkinson instantaneously snapped his fingers and he, his Warriors and the army of rat-humans were transported to the Other Realm, leaving Crawshaw where he stood...the gun in his hand still smoking.

The very second this happened, the police burst in and the three bullets with Atkinson's name on them embedded into Paul

Johnson's chest. The ex-policeman was catapulted back through the open door, and lay in agony as he bled on the steps.

"Arrest that man!" shouted Superintendent Malik. Her officers rushed to Crawshaw and restrained him. The entity within him left his body, passing through the police officers and into the wall. It was now without a life force and without its army of souls, all of which were now battling in the Other Realm.

Sergeant Glenn Simpson was the first to reach Paul Johnson as he lay dying on the steps of the mill. He had called for an ambulance just as Viktoria Malik arrived at his side.

"How is he?" she asked.

"He is unconscious, and I can't stop the bleeding," said Simpson.

Inside the mill, Chief Inspector Crawshaw stood dazed, confused, and handcuffed.

"What is happening?" he asked.

"I am arresting you on three...possibly five...counts of murder, attempted murder, suspicion of abduction, falsifying evidence and for your involvement in the mass suicide at the bridge. I caution you that anything you say will be written down, and may be used in evidence against you," said a solemn police officer.

"Murder? Attempted murder? What are you talking about, fool?!" said Crawshaw, regaining his senses somewhat.

"The murder of three officers at the police station on Park Road...unconfirmed reports of the murder of Miss Dixie Atkinson, the secretary at Atkinson, Dewhirst & Smith...and, by the looks of him as he left in the ambulance just now, the murder of ex-Chief Inspector Paul Johnson. Also, the attempted murder of Detective Chief Superintendent Viktoria Malik," said the arresting officer.

Viktoria Malik walked up to Crawshaw, looked him straight in the eyes, and said, "Take this piece of shit away!"

Chapter Fifteen

hief Inspector William Crawshaw had been read his rights, and was taken away to the police station to await an appearance in front of a judge. The dark souls from inside the old mill had materialised in a specially-prepared area of the Other Realm. At one end stood the disorganised, leaderless army of the Dark Realm; at the other end, Atkinson, Sarah, Gavin and Dixie stood with their swords drawn, and a single-minded intention for what was ahead of them.

The Dark Army realised they didn't need a leader as their enemies consisted of only four giants. They were thousands strong...albeit each one of them was only three or four feet tall. In total disarray, the Dark Hordes charged at the four giants. Atkinson shouted, "Sarah – to my left; Dixie – to my right! Sentinel, you have my back...are we ready?"

The word 'aye' came from his three Warriors, as the rat-humanoids encircled them.
"Everyone...take two steps forward to give yourself space to work in!" instructed Atkinson, the Warrior General.
Atkinson via Tamara linked his mind with the Reaper; the Reaper's mind linked with Paladin via Tamara; Tamara's mind linked with Dewhirst; Paladin's mind linked with Mother Nature, and Dewhirst's mind linked with Tamara and the Reaper of Rodentia.

Everything was in place as the rat-folk charged from all four directions.

On the Plane of Existence, the ambulance screeched to a halt outside of the hospital, and the paramedics rushed Paul Johnson inside. He was taken straight to the awaiting operating theatre, where the surgeon was already in situ.

"Let's have him on here," said the eminent surgeon Mr. Marcus Grant-Thomas, BS FRCS. "What do we have here, chaps?" he continued.

"Three bullet wounds to the chest; the patient has severe bradycardia, and his BP is 70/40."

"Okay boys and girls, we have to move fast...or we will lose him before we start."

In the Other Realm, the battle began, with the first of the Dark Army reaching the four mighty Warriors. Heads, arms, legs and torsos were flying everywhere, as the mighty blades of Atkinson's Warriors tore through the waves of rat-humans. The fear of weapons that Atkinson warned about proved to be unfounded. The Dark Realm had not produced any weapons at all, but there was a problem – as each Dark Soul was put to death, it seemed two more were taking its place. It was as if the portal was still open from that doomed realm, and more were streaming in. The sheer volume of rat-folk was becoming problematic.

Sarah's sword was unrelenting, simply swishing from side to side with no need of thrusting. The individual entities had no answers, but the volume of them was beginning to ask questions. The Sentinel stood strong, his strokes as strong as his wife's, disembowelling and beheading everything that came near his blade. Dixie held her flank with determined and telling sword-work, her concentration transfixed on the job at hand.

Atkinson stood solid and well in control of the situation, his blade leaving a trail of blood with its every cross and return.

In the Realm of Death, John Smith was tying and severing cords at breakneck speed of every creature that was passing through his Realm without even breaking into a sweat. Paladin was transferring the Dark Souls through the portal to Mother Nature, and the rats through Tamara to Dewhirst, who passed them to their Reaper.

Dewhirst noticed the large volumes of numbers being mentally passed around. He took advantage of the fact that he could hold time in the Great Room so he could check on Atkinson.

He materialised in the wings of the battle taking place, and saw the problem. He knew he had to stop the Hordes from coming through, but he also knew he couldn't leave any. With a wave of his hand, he changed into Warrior Mode and demanded every elemental within their Realm to take arms against their undiminishing foes.

Back at the police HQ, Detective Superintendent Viktoria Malik and the rest of her team were in a debriefing. With Crawshaw safely locked up in a cell, it was time for the thin blue line to congratulate itself on a job well done.

"There will be a lot of people both in and out of the police force who will be glad to see the back of Chief Inspector Crawshaw...me in particular. There is no room in the modern police force for individuals like him. We need more people like poor Mr. Johnson, and less of the likes of who replaced him. When all this has died down, I am going to root out personally as many homophobic, racist individuals from this police force as I can," said Viktoria Malik. The entire room of police officers cheered...with the exception of one, Police Officer Linda Harper, who just wanted to get her girlfriend home and begin a life together.

The battle raged on, all four Warriors now drenched in the blood of their foes, and that blood flowing in every direction like a river away from them. The ever-growing mound of corpses made it harder for them to see, but also, it was slowing down their opponents' rush towards them.

Atkinson noticed he was beginning to see that a gap was starting to form at the back of the battlefield, as Dewhirst's elementals began attacking the new arrivals. Hundreds of elementals were laying waste to thousands of rats infested with Dark Souls. Confident that his elementals were doing their job, Dewhirst left this area and headed for the Plane of Existence.

A sombre quiet fell amongst the medical staff on hand in the operating theatre as the surgeon finally stated the time, and pronounced that ex-Chief Inspector Paul Johnson was dead. A shadowy figure walked through Clive Thompson the anaesthetist and Wendy Walters the theatre sister to Johnson's side, and touched his wounds. Instantly, the beeps and buzzes were activated again, as the startled team of medics looked on in disbelief. On hearing the sounds, the surgeon looked back, then ran to the table.

"His BP is 120/60 and his pulse is 70 bpm!"
"Impossible!" said Marcus Grant-Thomas. "The man's dead!"
"It's not a mistake...just look at his chest...you can see him breathing!" gasped Wendy Walters, the theatre sister.
"Well, let's get the last of these bullets out...come on guys!" exclaimed the surgeon.

Dewhirst smiled and returned to the Other Realm and his desk, and the transferences began again.
In the Realm of Nature, the holding area was filling up – but instead of filling up with hateful souls, it was beginning to overflow with a powerful energy that brought hope for the future of the planet.

All the tormented souls passing through every part of this reaping process were cleansed, as they journeyed from Atkinson and his Warriors' swords to Smith in the Realm of Death, then onto Paladin on the Plane of Existence; the souls lost some of their negativity at each stage of the process. Finally, each soul passed through the Cleansing Portal into the Realm of Nature as pure Earth energy, and was accepted into the holding area by Mother Nature herself.

Within the Other Realm, Dewhirst's elementals had slain thousands of Dark Souls, as the battle-weary Warriors were dispatching the last few hundred to Smith, who in turn dispatched them to Paladin and Tamara. Dewhirst was now sitting back in his chair, dispatching the rats to their Reaper, who hadn't worked as hard in years.

As there were only a few Dark Souls left in front of Atkinson, his three Warriors came and stood at his side. All four were breathing heavily, and were covered head to toe in blood. Atkinson looked to his left at Sarah and Dixie, then to his right at Gavin, his Sentinel. He grinned, and to the sound of 'Charge!', all four screamed their ancient war cries. Swords forward, they ran at the last hundred or so Dark Souls, dispatching them in seconds with relative ease. With the battle won, the four bloodied Warriors were now the only ones standing, as the elementals had returned to their duties.

The battlefield was awash with bodies and blood. Atkinson drove his mighty sword into the ground. A ring of flames burst outwards across the devastation of that part of his very own realm, instantly setting fire to all the bodies that lay at the Warriors' feet. As the flames ravaged the deceased residents of the Dark Realm, Atkinson, Sarah, Dixie and Gavin walked through the fire and the flames and emerged clean and refreshed just outside Dewhirst's ornate doorway.

"Well done, everyone!" said Dewhirst.

"Thank you for your timely intervention," answered Atkinson.

Sarah was arm-in-arm with Gavin, another battle over, another battle won. Dewhirst looked at Dixie and said, "Go to your man." Dixie bowed her head, looked at her friends, and then depressed Paul Johnson's button on her phone.

She was shocked to materialise in the hospital, and in Intensive Care. Paul Johnson was lying on the bed asleep.

"My darling, what has happened!" exclaimed Dixie.

Paul Johnson awoke and said, "I had a bad day at the office dear, how did yours go?"

"It was bloody awful! Well, not really, but it was bloody. How did you end up in here?"

"Our Chief Inspector shot three rounds in my chest."

"Why did he shoot you?"

"He didn't – he shot at Atkinson. But as you guys left the party, the bullets with his name on them hit me...three times."

"It's a wonder it didn't kill you!" said Dixie.

"Oh, it did...but our Mr. Dewhirst came along and said hello. The next thing I knew, I was in this bed, as alive as ever."

Dixie leaned down and kissed him on his forehead, saying, "It's all over now, my darling. The Dark Realm is no more; we can get back to arranging our wedding."

"Yes – we don't want our son to be born out of wedlock, do we?" said Johnson.

"Our daughter will be born, whether we are married or not; she cannot be judged by a simple piece of paper. The true love and care bestowed upon her by her parents are what she needs."

"At last! You are pregnant, then! I had to be shot before you would finally tell me!" quipped Paul.

Dixie just giggled and said, "Of course I am, why do you think Atkinson sent us to that tropical island?"

"I thought it was for a well-deserved break."

"My love...Atkinson always has an ulterior motive. It was to produce Paladin's ocean counterpart, the Maiden of the Sea."

"Maiden of the Sea?" repeated Johnson.

"Yes, my love...finally the world will have balance. Aquallia will be the Water Element. Paladin is the Earth Element. Mother Nature is the air that we breathe, and Atkinson is the rejuvenating fire that purges. You see, Paul, the Earth will once again have elemental balance, so we will be able to be put things right...unlike when Atkinson's father ruled supreme, and anger, greed and war flourished."

"I take it we will need a house by the sea then?" said Johnson.

"Dewhirst is already having it built while we wait for the child's arrival."

"It's good to be an Immortal," said Johnson, as the nurse came in and explained to Dixie visiting time had ended hours ago.

In the Realm of Nature Paladin, astride Juliantrium, trotted up to Mother Nature, who was standing and admiring her new acquisition.

"A brilliant team effort, Paladin! It is the first time in many millennia that three Realms have worked together. The outcome was better than even I had anticipated! I feel reborn, and for the first time in a long time, I think I can trust an Atkinson again. Today's events have proven to be a great day for Humanity! It Is a shame they don't know anything about it," enthused Mother Nature.

"I feel strange," said Paladin.

"This is because your time is nigh," said Nature.

"My time?"

"Yes, Paladin...you will become Atkinson's Apprentice, and with me working my magic upon the Earth, you will learn from him how the humans live and die. You will learn their strengths and weaknesses, and he will show you your path, and to what end you will use your powers."

"When will this be?"

"Within the next twelve moons," said Mother Nature, as she turned once more to survey her cache of raw power.

In the Other Realm, Gavin and Sarah bid Atkinson and Dewhirst farewell for the time being, as they both returned to their penthouse apartment overlooking the City Centre. Alice was there to welcome them in from work, saying, "I have cooked dinner tonight, and there is a bottle of wine waiting for you in the lounge."

Sarah and Gavin stood on the balcony in each other's arms, looking at the night sky. Although they lived in the North of England, they were treated to a beautiful display of the Northern Lights – not the street lights, this was the Aurora Borealis right there, over Leeds. Gavin whispered into Sarah's ear, "I think Mother Nature must be pleased."

John Smith came from the Realm of Death after his mammoth shift and said, "Hi honey, I'm home!"

Tamara greeted him and said, "Well done, John, you were terrific...the Realm of Death is in good hands. Now, what do you want to do? Because I have heard, there is some fine Napoleon brandy about to be enjoyed, and I'm going to make my way there. You have a message from Tom Harper on your desk about your night out. Bye, sweetie!" she said, blowing him a kiss.

Picking up his phone, John Smith called Tom Harper. "Hi, Tom! I'm back from my travels, and would love to go out...do you fancy partying the night away? Because I sure do!"

"Sure! Do you mind if my sister and her new partner come along?" asked Tom.

"The more, the merrier," answered the Grim Reaper.

John Smith and Tom Harper met up with Linda Harper and Viktoria Malik outside the Viaduct pub, and all went inside. Sitting at their table, the two police officers wanted to talk about apprehending a crooked Police Chief Inspector. The Mortuary tech didn't want to talk about dissecting body parts, and the accountant thought it prudent not talk about his day at all, but a great time was had by everyone.

All over the world, baby rats were being born at a level never seen before. The rats were all disease-free, and ready to flourish in a world which would soon be a better place for their species, as animal testing would have no part in the Earth's imminent bright new future.

In the wall of the old mill just South of Leeds Lock, a shadow diminished into nothingness, and the Dark Realm truly died.

Atkinson and Dewhirst sat in their communal area, drinking a glass of rather fine brandy from Napoleon's private collection.

"Where can a lady get a decent drink around here?" said the beautiful woman who materialised in front of them.

Atkinson and Dewhirst both smiled at her, as the two Gods in their Valhalla were feeling quite pleased with themselves.

"A toast, my friends!" said Atkinson, pouring Tamara a drink. "To new beginnings!"

"To a brilliant team!" said Tamara.

"To Atkinson's Apprentice!" said Dewhirst.

"What!?" said Atkinson and Tamara.

JOHN PAUL BERNETT

The End...

...For Now

JOHN PAUL BERNETT

John Paul Bernett

JOHN PAUL BERNETT

John Paul Bernett

Be Happy